NICOLE MACCARRON

Hazel's Portal

Contents

Acknowledgement

Thank you to my Beta Readers Sara and Ian, who saved the day when my deadline was looming. Thank you for your help and advice! Thank you to Sara Oliver Designs for yet another fantastic book cover. And thank you to Sarah Hawkins for entertaining me with your editing comments while gently pushing me to improve. I appreciate you all!

1

Chapter 1: Kelly

Sixteen Months Ago

The floor was cold under Kelly's crossed legs. Her eyes were closed, and her face was wet with tears. She could feel the chilly wind on her bare arms and knew it signalled a change. She had left her sister, Hazel, sitting on the floor of their mother's bedroom, and entered the afterlife. With a trembling breath, she opened her eyes. She was in the middle of her high school's empty hallway, roughly where she had died. The familiar lockers lined both walls. It was dark in the absence of the fluorescent overhead lights, and piles of leaves skittered across the floor like rats. Her lip curled in disappointment. Some afterlife.

Kelly rose to her feet and turned in a circle. Her mouth dropped open. Behind her was an open door in the lockers, where no door ought to be. A thin sheet of light poured down the length of the doorway, glowing and dripping like bioluminescent water. The water glowed an electric purple. Through the water was Hazel. She was looking around their mother's room with grief etched across her face. Kelly's heart leapt at the sight of her. What if it wasn't goodbye after all?

Her head swimming with giddy relief, Kelly reached out to part the sheet of water, but a Shadow flashed across the hallway on her right. Kelly yelped. Her eyes darted from wall to wall, floor to ceiling, but she couldn't see anyone. Hardly daring to breathe, she took a step down the hallway, trying to see into the distance. She strained her ears for footsteps.

The purple light disappeared, plunging Kelly into darkness. She whirled back to look at the portal. There was nothing in front of her but lockers.

"No!" she gasped. She pressed her hands against the lockers, rattling the locks in her frantic search for the door.

"Welcome to the next layer," a voice said from the left.

Kelly screamed and whirled around, her back against the wall.

"Sorry!" the voice cried.

She clutched her heart. In front of her stood a boy of roughly her own age. She looked him up and down as her heartbeat slowed. He had a slim build with the warm brown skin of a red cedar tree, and he wore a simple white t-shirt with jeans. He raised his hands in apology.

"You scared me!" Kelly snapped. She swiped at her face with the short sleeve of her t-shirt, drying her tears.

"I'm sorry," he said again, cringing as he scratched above his ear where his close-cropped black hair met with longer curls. He groaned. "This is already going worse than I planned."

Kelly narrowed her eyes. She glanced back down the hallway where she'd seen the Shadow. There was still nothing there. She fixed her glare back on the boy.

"What are you?" she demanded.

"What—what am I?" he stuttered as if he hadn't quite heard

her right. "I'm a dead guy, just like you. I mean, not that you're a guy, you're a girl—or are you? I don't mean to assume—I mean, I'm just–just not alive."

He fell into a sheepish silence but offered a smile, the red in the cedar skin of his cheeks growing more pronounced.

When she didn't return the smile, he offered his hand instead. "I'm Logan."

Kelly didn't take it.

Logan let his hand drop. "Well," he said, clearly determined to win her over, "I've been waiting for you. Not in a creepy way!" he assured her, laughing a little too loud. He cut himself off with a cough. "Just that I've been here a really long time. Or at least I think I have. It's hard to tell. Anyway, I haven't been able to go on like everyone else. I've been waiting for something. Someone. And I think that someone is you!"

He beamed at her like she was some kind of hero. Kelly didn't care how long he had been waiting, and she didn't care about his disarming manner either. Something wasn't right here, and she was wasting time talking to him.

She left Logan standing there. Keeping close to the walls, she jogged on tiptoe down the hallway in the direction the Shadow had gone.

Logan came scrambling after her. "Where are you going?"

"What was that thing?" she whispered instead.

"The door?"

"No, the Shadow."

She reached a corner and peered around it. At the end of the hall stood an exterior door sandwiched by narrow windows. A dim beam of light pierced the darkness. The door was open a crack as if someone had just passed by. It creaked in the chilly air and more leaves rolled into the corners of the hall, wrestling in the autumn breeze.

With no Shadow in sight, Kelly marched to the door and threw it open, stepping out into the sunlight. The front lawn was deserted. A few more paces and she could see that the parking lot was empty too. Not one car passed on the road in front of the school. Her eyes landed on the trees, which were orange and red. The ones she had just left behind were summertime green. Goosebumps rose on her arms.

Kelly rounded on Logan. "What is this place? Where is everyone?"

"Well," Logan said, "I think of it as the next layer. Because I think it's sort of on top of our old reality."

"How do you know that?"

"I don't." He gestured at the school and grounds. "I played soccer here a few times, so I know it's a real place. But it's not the same as before. It's like you said, where is everyone? It's the same, but it's not."

Kelly strode to the nearest tree and patted its bark. It felt real. Unexpected tears came to her eyes. She could interact with this world, unlike when she was a ghost in the last one. Logan came up beside her and put his hand through the tree.

"Pretty cool, huh?" he said, misinterpreting her misty eyes for wonder. "You can do it too. Go on, try it."

Kelly stroked the bark with gentle fingers, and their tips disappeared into the tree. She sighed. Exhaustion hit her.

"So, my sister is in the other layer? The old one?"

Logan's expression sobered. He didn't need to say more.

Kelly swallowed. "Will ... will she come here when she dies?"

Logan hesitated and said, "I'm no expert. I haven't spoken to anyone since I've been here. Not really. They pass right through too fast. Until you, that is."

She met his eye and saw hope there. It was painful to look at. She wondered how long he had been alone. Kelly dropped her gaze and took a step back, folding her arms.

"Are there shadows here?" she asked point blank.

"Shadows?" Logan's gaze went to their own shadows on the grass.

"I saw something when I first arrived. Something moved in the hallway."

"Oh, that's just another soul. They pass through fast."

It dawned on Kelly that Hazel had been saying goodbye to both her and Alexis, another dead friend. Maybe the shadow Kelly saw was just Alexis passing through. But then, why hadn't Kelly passed through?

"Where do the other souls go?" she asked.

Logan's eyes lit up. "Oh, you have to see it. Follow me!"

2

Chapter 2: Hazel

N^{ow} Hazel hummed as she wafted lavender smoke across the bed she shared with Jen. Sunbeams illuminated the smoke through the second-story window, but the glass was shut tight against autumn's chilly approach. Three urns sat on the windowsill, each shining a different colour as the sun gleamed against the ceramic. Downstairs, the sound of dishes clattering announced Jen's turn to cook for their housemates, both of whom were studying in the living room. It was the perfect time for Hazel to cleanse the upstairs.

Opening her closet, Hazel pushed aside her clothes and watched the smoke curl over a sign tucked in the very back. The words on the sign announced, 'Hazel Connors: Medium.' When the smoke had touched everything, she smiled and closed the folding doors again.

A bubbly pop song interrupted her peaceful chore, and Hazel cursed her phone's timing. With the stalk of burning lavender in one hand, she set her phone on the nightstand, hit speaker, and answered.

"Hello, is this Hazel Connors? I'm looking to book an appointment—"

"Oh, I'm sorry," Hazel interrupted before the caller could go on. "I don't do that anymore."

"Oh. Oh, no. I was really hoping to speak to my brother—"

"Yeah, I'm sorry to disappoint you," Hazel said. "But I hope you find the right person to help you. And I'm sorry for your loss. Really. Good luck."

"But—"

"Take care," Hazel said and hung up. She chewed her lip for a moment, staring at the photo of her and Jen on the main screen. Then she gave her head a little shake and went back to cleansing.

***

There was one last job to do. Padding down the stairs, Hazel entered the living room, where Riva was lying on the couch with a textbook over her face. Kate was cross-legged on the hardwood floor, typing on a laptop near the only remaining outlet.

She glanced up at Hazel and grumbled, "We need a carpet over here; the floor's freezing."

Hazel grinned. "Just wear pants."

"I will not," Kate scoffed. "Shorts and sweaters 'til it snows."

"I didn't know you were so dedicated to looking cute."

Kate rolled her heavily kohled eyes and continued typing. "You want to unpack my winter crap?"

Hazel ignored her. "Speaking of cute," she said, lifting the textbook off Riva's face to expose her open-mouthed nap.

Riva snorted awake. "Mmm? What?"

"History still fascinating?" Kate smirked over her shoulder.

"Done with that essay?" Riva shot back.

The smirk slipped off Kate's face and she glowered at the laptop. Hazel laughed.

"You're in a good mood," Riva noted, sitting up.

Hazel shrugged and looked across the stairs to where Jen was cooking in the kitchen. "You know I love when she cooks. Anyway, I'm about to cleanse my car and I was wondering if you want me to do yours?"

Riva yawned. "Is that necessary?"

"You'd think so if you ever looked in the rearview and saw someone sitting in the backseat."

Riva shuddered. "Yes, please."

Kate rose in one smooth motion and followed Hazel out the front door, shivering against the chill.

"So you're doing ghost stuff today?" she asked, eyes shining.

"The opposite, actually. I'm keeping them away."

Kate was so close on Hazel's heels that Hazel almost hit her with the car door.

"But we could do the travelling tonight, couldn't we?" Kate went on.

Hazel heaved a long-suffering sigh as she sparked her lighter. "Kate, you're procrastinating again."

"I'm not!"

Hazel tilted her head.

"Okay, just a little, but so what?"

Hazel sat in the front seat of her old beater and began wafting the lavender over the dashboard. "You say that, but you'd lose a whole night."

Kate folded her arms. "You told me you'd show me how to use the cords."

Hazel tried to keep her face impassive as she searched for

more excuses. "It might not work for you."

"I know."

A gust of wind sent leaves twirling down from the maple tree at the foot of the yard and Kate rubbed her arms for warmth.

Hazel smiled. "Finish your essay, unpack your clothes, and then ask me again."

"But that could be weeks!"

Hazel grinned at the steering wheel.

"Touché, you wicked woman," Kate said with narrowed eyes. She threw her arms to the sky and cried, "Grant me patience!" before stomping back into the house.

Hazel glanced around to make sure the neighbours weren't watching before she moved to the backseat with her lavender. To her surprise, a curvy blonde-haired woman was standing under the maple tree, waving her over. Judging by the look of distress on her face, Hazel guessed that this woman wasn't a neighbour. She pointed to the lavender in her other hand and gave an apologetic shrug. Then she turned her back on the ghost.

***

Dinner was a noisy affair as the four girls sat around the creaky kitchen table and dove into the rice bowls Jen had prepared.

Riva raised her glass. "To our first roommates' dinner!"

"It still feels illegal," Jen laughed.

"Cheers!" The others grinned, clinking their glasses.

"And to Jen, for an excellent warm meal," Hazel added.

"Here, here!" Kate agreed.

"I'm glad you like it," Jen said. "Let me know if it's too spicy. I only used a little less than my mom does."

All around the table the girls shouted her down, despite Kate's

9

nose starting to run and a flush climbing her cheeks. Then the doorbell rang and Riva rose to answer. Her dad greeted the girls from the doorway.

"Hi, Jermaine!" Hazel called from the table as he embraced Riva.

"Hazel," he nodded, the corner of his lip quirking up. "Good to see you." He held out a textbook for Riva. "I'm just dropping off Riva's book."

"We have extra," Jen offered.

Jermaine shook his head. "Thank you, but I've got to get Derrick to soccer practice."

Hazel and Riva's adopted brother stuck his head in and waved. Hazel grinned at the 11-year-old.

"Have fun!" Hazel called to him.

"Bye, Dad," Riva said as they departed. "Thanks!"

She set the textbook down on the kitchen counter and bounced back to her seat.

"So, I'm happy to report our first month of rent is paid on time," Riva said, her chair giving a scrape of approval as she tucked it in. "Thank you, everyone, for being so on top of it."

Riva, Hazel, and Jen had moved into the house at the start of September, but Kate was a new addition.

"Cleansing is also done for the month," Hazel said, "so I can guarantee us a ghost-free thirty days or so."

"And I'm almost done unpacking," Kate announced.

Jen almost choked on her drink.

"No, I'm really not," Kate grinned as Hazel and Riva laughed.

"Do you ever plan to fully move in?" Jen asked, rolling her eyes.

Kate's belongings had been trickling in all month, and now her room was stacked with so many cardboard boxes she could barely squeeze past. Yesterday Riva had tripped over a box in the hallway and almost fell down the stairs.

"Hey, if I'd been invited before the semester started ...," Kate joked, giving a hearty sniff. "But actually, Hazel made me a deal today, so I'm feeling pretty motivated."

"Oh? What deal is this?" Jen asked.

"Yeah," Hazel agreed through a forkful of food. "What deal?"

"That you'll show me how to use the cords if I finish my essay and unpack."

"That—no—" Hazel sputtered as Jen and Riva exchanged looks. "That's not what I meant."

"We agreed, no ghost stuff in our shared home," Jen said, frowning. "This is supposed to be our safe space."

"It's technically not ghost stuff," Kate argued. "We're just going to contact Riley."

"Ghost stuff meaning supernatural stuff," Jen corrected. She rubbed the scars on her neck. "The last thing we need is another ... this summer."

"Can't you use a phone?" Riva teased.

Kate pouted. "I just want to know if I can do it."

Hazel cleared her throat. "I think we have to take into account what Jen and Riva are saying here. They need to feel safe in their own home."

"Where are we supposed to do it then? A graveyard?"

No one cracked a smile. Hazel's hand rose to grasp the pendant hanging on her necklace. It was a thin glass vial with a cork stopper. She had found it online and had stuffed a sprig of dried lavender inside. It didn't work as well as smoke to keep ghosts at bay, but Hazel had discovered that it bought her some distance, especially if she uncorked the lid. She doubted it would be strong enough in a graveyard.

Kate took in all their serious faces and slumped.

"Sorry, Kate," Hazel said, "but it *is* best not to mess with this stuff."

***

Hazel usually slept soundly after a cleansing day, but tonight she found herself staring at Jen's hair. Jen was sleeping curled up on her side, her hair fanned out on the pillow behind her. The purple dye was fading from her thick brown locks. It was now the exact shade of the lavender in Hazel's necklace.

Hazel sighed and rolled onto her back. Hazel had tempted fate one too many times, and had almost lost Jen in the process. In fact, if Hazel never saw another ghost again, she would be happy. Unfortunately, Kate was both persistent and fascinated by the supernatural. This conversation was far from over.

A car beam illuminated the little room as it drove past. When it was gone, the shadows in the room had changed. A jolt went through Hazel. People surrounded her bed, their faces indistinct in the darkness. Her hand, inches from the sleeping Jen, couldn't move to shake her awake. Her lungs were frozen.

The people were all poised the same way, with one or two hands raised in front of their chests as if pulling something. The moment Hazel realized what it was, blue light blinded her. Glowing cords stretched from each of their hearts to hers.

Another car passed, and in the beam of its headlights, all the figures silently mouthed, "Run, Hazel."

Then they were gone.

3

Chapter 3: Riley

Riley had been having a stress dream about school when a new, pitch-black room invaded his thoughts, pushing out the old dream. His stomach clenched with dread. He stared into the dream corner, waiting for the darkness to move. There was a shimmer, the glistening of a woman's eyes as she stepped towards him.

"Run," she said.

There was a creak in the ceiling over Riley's head. He opened his eyes, his heart beating a frantic rhythm against his ribs. He had escaped her early this time. Riley let out a long breath. He sat up in bed, a book falling from his chest to the mattress, and stared up at the ceiling. A growl to his left announced the arrival of Charlie, Riley's Saint Bernard German-Sheppard. His hackles rose as he stared up at the ceiling.

"Mom!" Riley called, rubbing his face. "There's a raccoon in the roof again!"

Elisabeth came stomping down the hall. "Not again!"

She paused in the doorway, and they both froze, listening. After a minute of silence, she dropped her crossed arms.

"If you hear it again, let me know. I'll have to get some more traps."

Riley nodded and stretched. He grabbed some clothes from a pile on the floor, shifting a package he had opened and forgotten. It was a tiny pendant necklace Hazel had recommended. He had yet to buy lavender to stuff inside, so back to the floor it had gone in the meantime. When he looked back up, Elisabeth was still standing in the doorway.

"Did you sleep last night?"

Riley shook his head and shifted the blankets behind him to cover the book he had been reading.

"Did you ... see anything?" she asked.

Riley bit his cheek. It was the same old question: Had he seen his dad's ghost?

"No," he said, flattening his hair. "It was just nightmares."

"Well," she said, breezing past the moment, "maybe we should think about getting you some sleeping pills. And it's definitely time to limit screens an hour before bedtime."

Riley suppressed an eye roll, but barely. He had no problem falling asleep. It was staying asleep after seeing the woman that was the problem. Lately he had given up entirely and resorted to reading.

"I'll call the doctor today," Elisabeth went on. She tousled his flattened hair, and Riley grimaced at her. "What's your plan?"

"Wyatt and I are helping set up the dance, so I'm going to his place and we're walking over."

Elisabeth smiled. Riley was back in touch with his old friend, and he was taking on some new responsibilities at school this year. He had said all the right things.

"Okay," she said, watching him straighten his hair again. "Do you have your clothes picked out?"

Riley shrugged. He didn't want to admit how long it took to select the navy-blue collared shirt and black jeans. Just the right combination of dressed up and casual.

"Okay," she said again. "Call me if you need anything. Be good. No fights this year."

Riley huffed out a laugh and agreed. "No fights."

***

As he walked over to Wyatt's house, a cool October wind chilled his nose and lifted the hair from Riley's forehead. It was almost time for gloves. He was about to see Sophie at the dance, where she was the head organizer, but Riley let his fingers suffer in order to text Sophie about the book they were both reading. Between volunteering and showing an interest in her books, Riley hoped he could win back some of the credit that had been ripped out from under him last year. Sophie had been caught in the cross fire when two bullies had picked a fight with him.

Despite the bags under his eyes, he arrived at Wyatt's house with buoyed spirits after Sophie's excited response, "I can't wait to pick your brain about it!"

Wyatt opened the door, took one look at Riley, and said, "If I looked like that, I wouldn't be grinning."

"Shut up," Riley laughed, shoving past him.

Riley inhaled the delicious aroma of fried bread as they made their way to the downstairs rec room, where Wyatt had paused his video game. A plate of bannock sat on the coffee table, and Riley helped himself as he dropped onto the saggy couch.

"Did you have that dream again?" Wyatt asked.

"Yeah."

"Did you try your friend's trick with the lavender?"

"Not yet," Riley said, propping his feet on the coffee table, but careful not to upend the plate. "I'm pretty sure that only works for ghosts anyway, not for dreams."

"So you think it was just a dream then?"

Riley chewed while studying the pause screen for a moment before he answered. "I can't shake the feeling that it's more than that. It looks real. The way the shadows move on her face …" He shivered.

Wyatt grimaced. "So you haven't slept in like four nights? Maybe it's time to ask your friend if she's ever experienced anything like this."

Riley rubbed the back of his neck. "Good point. Only problem is, she asked for space from the whole ghost thing. She's in university, you know, so she's trying to concentrate."

Wyatt reached for his controller on the coffee table and tossed the other to Riley. "She's your friend. I'm sure she'll want to help with this. Now die before we have to dance."

Riley laughed and set to chasing down Wyatt's avatar.

***

Riley thought the decorations in the school gym looked pretty pathetic. He had spent all afternoon stringing vines all over the walls, and he was sweating through his carefully chosen clothes. Then another volunteer turned the lights off and someone else plugged in the twinkle lights. It turned out the fluorescents had not been doing them any favours. In the dark, the lights gave off a moody glow that suggested stars peeking through the jungle canopy. He glanced over at Sophie, who was surveying the jungle theme with an approving smile. He caught her eye and grinned.

"Okay, volunteers, great job!" the Leadership teacher called out. "Now come get your pizza!"

Riley sidled up to Sophie as the group cheered and made their way to the cafeteria.

"It looks great in there," he said, finding himself unexpectedly breathless.

"Doesn't it?" she said, giving him a glowing smile. "I can't wait for everyone to see!"

"Yeah, you're really good at designing this stuff," Riley said. He had to bite his lip to make space for her response instead of spilling too many compliments. Like how cute she was.

Sophie blushed and tucked her long brown hair behind her ears. "Thank you. I really appreciate all your help. I know you could have been reading."

Riley laughed, but stopped abruptly when it was too much. They took seats together in the cafeteria, Wyatt and a few of Sophie's friends joining them. Riley spent most of the meal eating. Sophie's presence beside him was like a wave pulling him into the ocean, taking all his attention and deafening him to other conversations. Too soon, the girls stood and announced they were going to go change.

"But you look..." Riley trailed off.

Sophie's face reddened at his unspoken words, and the other girls dragged her away, giggling. Riley cringed and dropped his forehead to the table when they were out of sight.

"It's not all bad," Wyatt said. Riley looked up to see him grinning. "I saw her smile. She likes you, man."

***

Riley and Wyatt waited in the lobby for the gym to fill up. Music was already drifting out the gym doors, but neither of them were up to dancing yet. At last, Riley spotted Sophie bouncing into the lobby in a pink, off-the-shoulder dress. Her cheeks were radiant with some kind of shimmering powder, and her excited smile lit her face. She locked eyes with Riley and her smile faltered. Riley's heart stuttered. Did she not want to see him?

"Wave, you dipshit," Wyatt muttered.

Riley lifted his hand as if Wyatt were controlling his strings. Sophie's smile returned and she hurried to join them.

"Ready?" she asked, taking both boys by the elbow.

She took a deep breath as if bracing herself for everyone to hate the dance. Then she led the boys and her friends into the flashing lights of the gym.

In no time at all, the dance floor was crowded and sweltering hot. Riley couldn't wipe the smile off his face when he found himself next to Sophie without much effort. It was so dark and busy that no one could really judge his dance moves, so Riley relaxed into the music. After a while, though, Riley pulled at his collar, the warmth, physical exertion, and sheer exhaustion all beginning to add up. He was panting like he'd been running and he couldn't quite get a deep enough breath.

"I'll be right back," he shouted to Sophie. He squeezed his way between all the flailing arms before she could reply, and escaped through the back exit.

Just as he hit the fresh air, the music changed, and Riley hesitated. It was a slow song. Part of him wanted to sprint back in and seize his opportunity to dance with Sophie. The other part tensed at the very idea. He stood frozen for a minute with his back to the partnering crowd behind him. Then he stepped outside into the bracing night air. Sophie would probably have a partner before he even made it back. Swallowing his disappointment, Riley found a blank piece of wall to lean against and fanned his shirt to cool off.

A surge of students poured out the door beside him, all fleeing the pressure of the slow song. A few girls shivered in their sleeveless dresses. Everyone else let out predictable sighs of relief as they milled about the parking lot. Riley closed his eyes.

"Hazel?" a muffled voice called.

Riley tilted his head at the familiar name, thinking his ears had gone funny from the loud music.

"Hazel!" the voice called again.

Riley stepped an inch away from the wall to see who was speaking. He didn't know any Hazels at this school. The voice seemed to be coming from the gym, but if it was, he shouldn't have been able to hear it so clearly over the music. He stepped in front of the door and his eyes popped. He was not looking at the jungle vines and flowers. He saw only the darkened and deserted gym, leaves drifting across the floor, and a girl, her mouth falling open at the sight of him. He blinked hard, wondering if he had wandered off somewhere and forgotten, but no, she was still there. He glanced left and right, but the people outside were still chatting as if nothing had changed.

"Hey!" the girl said in her blurred voice. She darted towards the door, but then slammed into an invisible surface, like a sliding glass door. Her brown hair swung back with the force of it.

"Oh!" Riley said aloud, racing forwards to help her.

She held out a hand to hold him off and pinched her nose with the other. "I'm fine," she said, while a trail of blood dripped towards her upper lip.

She put her free hand on the surface, and her palm flattened. The air she touched rippled like a pool of water. He met her eyes, which were watering with pain. The colour of her dark blue irises looked familiar. Riley reached for the surface, too, but all at once it was gone. He blinked, and sound came back. Two boys stood in front of him trying to get outside for fresh air, but Riley was blocking their path.

"Move," Aaron said, as courteous as ever.

Riley remembered the feel of Aaron's face under his fist last year and let it comfort him. He took a minuscule step to the side and waved Aaron and Mason past with a dead expression. They moved on without another word. At least they weren't picking fights anymore.

Riley surreptitiously raised a hand to make sure he could pass through the doorway before stepping back into the flashing lights. The slow song was just ending. Many of the students had taken their conversations to the walls. To Riley's surprise, Sophie was leaning against the wall a short distance away, one hand on the crook of her other elbow. Her expression was aloof, but the way her eyes kept scanning the crowd made his stomach twinge with guilt.

He backed into the shadows, a few eleventh graders separating him from Sophie. What had he just seen? He was sure the girl had said Hazel's name, but surely she was searching for a different Hazel. Then again, what were the chances he would stumble upon another Hazel who was involved with strange, supernatural things?

Riley closed his eyes for a moment and felt himself sway. He jerked upright and glanced around to make sure no one had noticed. The realization dawned on him. He was exhausted to the point of hallucinating. His nightmares had kept him up four nights in a row, and then he had spent his remaining energy dancing. He needed to go home.

He lurched forwards to find Wyatt, rubbing his eyes. The music had changed, and students were flooding the floor again.

"There you are," Sophie said, appearing at his elbow.

"Yeah," Riley answered, forcing a smile as he searched for his ride home. "Have you seen Wyatt?"

"There," Sophie said, pointing to the middle of the crowd.

Riley sighed and began dodging arms as he made his way to Wyatt's side. Sophie followed in his wake. Wyatt was grinning and shouting something into the ear of one of Sophie's friends.

"Hey!" Riley called. "I have to go."

"What?"

"I have to go!"

"No, you can't go yet!" Sophie's friend cried.

The smile slipped off Wyatt's face when he saw Riley's serious expression. "Just a minute," he said to her, and followed Riley out of the throng.

In the lobby, where they could actually hear each other, Riley said, "I can't stay awake anymore. I'm literally hallucinating. I need to go home."

Wyatt's brow furrowed with concern. "Okay. I'll go tell the girls you aren't feeling well."

Riley slid down the wall with a grateful nod.

***

He couldn't keep his eyes open in the car. The woman's face loomed out of the darkness, and Riley's veins turned to ice.

"Don't go home," she whispered.

Riley jolted awake and put his head in his hands.

"Just sleep," Wyatt said as he navigated the darkened streets. "There's no shame in it."

Riley shook his head. "It's not that. It's that woman."

Wyatt's mouth dropped open in alarm. "That's messed up, man."

"I don't know what to do," Riley moaned.

"Well, you have to do something," Wyatt said. "She's not giving you a minute of peace. You're a mess. Have you tried telling her to go to hell?"

Riley laughed through his nose. "Next time."

When they pulled up in front of his house, Riley climbed out like his body was made of lead.

"Thanks, Wyatt. And sorry."

"Don't worry about it," Wyatt said. "I hope you sleep for a week."

Riley chuckled again, shut the car door, and made his way up the drive. He shivered from more than just the cold air.

Inside, Riley kicked off his shoes as Elisabeth sat upright on the couch, her eyebrows rising.

"You're back early! I wasn't expecting you for at least another hour. How was the dance?"

"Good, but I'm beat. I'm going to bed."

Elisabeth blocked him halfway across the living room and wrapped him in a hug. "Okay, sweetheart. I love you."

Riley sank into her embrace, ready to fall asleep in her arms. "Love you too."

He stumbled to his room and lay down fully clothed on top of his covers. He knew what image would plague him as soon as he closed his eyes. Riley thought of the girl he had seen smashing into the air instead. Hallucination or not, he decided to try reaching out to her.

Closing his eyes, he mentally felt for the cords that stretched from his heart out into the world. He sifted through them, trying to sense if one belonged to the girl, but nothing stood out. Maybe this was proof she wasn't real. He opened his eyes again and repositioned to climb under his blankets, only to freeze. He was looking down at his own body.

4

Chapter 4: Kelly

Sixteen Months Ago

Kelly jogged to keep up with Logan as he led her down the city streets. He was breathless with excitement.

"It took me a long time to find this place," he said. "Or I think it did. Like I said, time is weird here—" He cut himself off. "Oh, look, there goes a soul now."

A door had opened ahead of them in the middle of the street. Kelly jerked to a stop. Through the door, she could see a desert road in stark contrast to the green Canadian city that surrounded them. This time, the water-like air in the door was blue. A man stood on the other side, but when he stepped through the frame, he emerged as a whirl of muted colours. The water-like air in the portal rippled behind him. As if caught in a fast-flowing river, his colours flew down the street, twisting and drifting.

"Come on!" Logan cried, and he stepped into the air to race after them.

Kelly's mouth dropped open. Logan was flying as easily as if

23

he had climbed some stairs into the sky.

Kelly ran after him. "How did you do that?"

"Oh!" Logan laughed, stopping in midair to float before her as she caught up. "Well, it's just like it looks. To get started, you pretend there's something to step on. Then you're just doing it!"

She looked up at him with raised eyebrows, then back at the pavement. Stranger things had happened in Kelly's last month than this. She tested her foot on the air, but her sole found pavement again. She glanced at Logan, who nodded encouragingly. The door on the street was already gone, and the man who had transformed into colours was disappearing around a corner.

Her eyes narrowed at Logan. Kelly didn't trust him not to laugh at her. She broke into a run, following the colours, pushing herself faster and faster, her arms pumping and breath panting.

"Hey!" Logan called behind her.

Just as she reached top speed, Kelly leapt into the air like she was skipping several steps in a flight of stairs. Her feet pumped to keep running in midair. To her astonishment, both feet met something solid, which she pushed off. She was soaring, running on air. Kelly gasped, her stomach flipping with the speed of it. It felt like she was still running on pavement, but she could see the specks of grey rock speeding by several feet under her. Her heart almost burst with joy as the chilly wind blasted back her hair.

Logan caught up to her, laughing. "Well, that's one way to do it!"

Whether Logan deserved trust or not, Kelly's smile was out of her control. She turned her gaze back to the street down below, which zoomed past as if she could see out the bottom of a car. With only a thought, she rose higher. Now she was flying over the orange-coloured trees that lined the street. Her eyes welled with the beauty of it all, the wind whipping away her tears.

A minute later, Logan was calling for her to slow down, but Kelly didn't want to. She wanted to pass the buildings of the city and fly across the oceans she had never had a chance to visit in life. She wanted to soar over mountains and rivers and take in all the beauty this second chance offered.

"Don't you want to see where they go?" Logan called.

As curiosity came back to her, Kelly's speed slowed and her height lowered. Without much conscious effort, she was within stepping distance to the ground. She descended the remaining few feet like stairs and found her feet back on the ground.

"You figured that out much faster than I did," Logan admitted, rubbing his neck.

He pointed to the building in front of them. They had landed in a parking lot before a one-story building. To the left was a park with a wide pond and a fountain in the middle.

"The library?" Kelly asked in disbelief. "Ghosts go to the library?"

"I think it's poetic," Logan said, his expression turning dreamy. "What are books anyway but a different layer of reality?"

He left Kelly standing there and headed down the path to the front door. She couldn't argue with him. Kelly had always felt that when she read a book, she was in two worlds at once. Putting a hand through a tree earlier was a weirdly similar experience, really. She hurried to catch up with his long strides.

Logan moved through the door without opening it, and Kelly followed. Like everywhere else, the inside was deserted. They padded over the linoleum of the lobby and onto the worn grey carpet of the shelving area. Most of the bookshelves were metal, but Logan was leading Kelly to her favourite part of the library: the teen section. Here they found two rows of heavy oak shelves with a door of books fastening them together on one end. Logan opened the bookshelf door and they passed through a hidden tunnel of paperbacks into the teen section. At the end of the aisle, they emerged into a dim rectangular room of wall-to-wall books and scattered bean bag chairs. There was only one other exit, a door that had been papered to look like a shelf. But for the push handle and glowing exit sign, it could easily be missed.

"What are we doing here?" Kelly asked.

"Do you feel that?" Logan replied.

Kelly looked askance at him, but then she noticed a tingling in her feet. The more she focused on it, the stronger it seemed to get, until it became a call to move. As soon as Kelly acted on it, she saw what Logan had brought her here for. Two more doors appeared in the far shelves, straight ahead. Side-by-side, they towered over Kelly. Neither frame had a door, but stood open and inviting. Kelly's whole body began to tingle as she stared into their depths, resisting the urge to race through.

"Where do they go?" Kelly whispered.

"On," Logan said simply, "I think."

Kelly could feel the certainty in herself as well, like a blanket wrapped around her shoulders, or a monster waiting under the bed. She could see nothing in the left door. It was black as a night without stars, but something in her cried out for the nothingness, begging for relief, for rest. She tore her eyes away and studied the other. This portal was made of silvery colours, like the ghost they had seen earlier. The colours swirled like the sheen on a bubble, and reminded Kelly of childhood and joy. She smiled, but the smile slipped as she listened to the faint musical hum coming from its depths. It was beautiful and low, the sound of dread. She frowned, her chest tightening.

"Which door?" Logan asked softly.

Kelly took another step closer. "Which door?" she repeated in a daze.

An ominous rushing sound tore through the main library. Kelly and Logan both turned to stare down the aisle behind them, then met each other's eyes. Logan looked unnerved, which was enough to tell Kelly no one else should be here. She stepped away from the doors, and only then realized the magnetic pull she was under. Her steps took more effort than on the way in. The pull she had been feeling was not so gentle after all. With a surge of effort, she broke free and jogged down the row of books to push the secret door open a crack.

Not a page rustled in the main library. It appeared as silent and deserted as before. She squinted down the aisles, expected to see someone staring back at her. Then a door slammed. Kelly squealed and clamped a hand over her mouth.

Logan pushed the secret door farther so they could peer around it together. To the left was the door that had slammed. It was a new door that Kelly had never seen before. It matched the other library doors, but it had crashed shut so forcefully that cracks snaked their way along the library walls and up into the ceiling. Yet even as they watched, the library seemed to send tendrils of its own into the door. The colours of the surrounding books and shelves bled over the door's surface until it blended back into the library. The door was being erased.

When it had disappeared completely, Kelly and Logan tugged the secret door shut.

5

Chapter 5: Hazel

N^{ow} It was 11:00pm, and Hazel sat on the couch in the dark with a blanket over her legs. The remaining sprigs of lavender were burning in a seashell on the coffee table and she was hiding behind the smoke.

There was no way ghosts could have gotten into her bedroom. Hazel pulled the blanket higher to her chest. It was people who had visited her. People who knew about cords. People like her, who could get into her house uninvited.

There was a creak on the stairs, and Hazel's head jerked in that direction. Kate emerged at the bottom, tiptoeing.

"You're still up?" Hazel asked.

Kate let out a small yelp and raised a fist as if to fend Hazel off.

"It's just me!" Hazel said, leaning around the stream of smoke so Kate could see her.

Kate clutched her heart. There was an empty glass in her other hand. "I thought you went to bed an hour ago!"

"I did."

Kate sidled into the living room, eyeing the smoke. "What are you doing?"

Hazel hesitated. If she told the truth now, she would shatter the apparent illusion that they were safe from ghosts in their own home. Then again, Kate had been in favour of ghosts at dinnertime.

"Well ...," she began, and explained all about the people with the cords.

"Are you sure they said 'run'?" Kate was sitting on the couch now, knees swaddled in a blanket of her own. None of the girls felt safe with their feet on the floor these days.

Hazel shrugged. "That's what it looked like."

Kate let out a low whistle. "So what are you going to do?"

"I could try to find them ... But the only person I've ever looked for that I didn't know was Riley. Well, him and the Shadow ..."

They exchanged tense looks.

"And I did promise not to mess with this stuff for a while," Hazel added.

"I'm sure Jen and Riva would understand if you explained."

Hazel fiddled with a hole in the blanket. "It's not just that. I need to concentrate on my school work too ..."

"And?" Kate prompted.

"And I deserve a break," Hazel said, parroting some of Jen's words.

Kate wasn't fooled. She raised an eyebrow.

Hazel watched the smoke spiral to the ceiling before answering. "And I'm scared."

Kate nodded, hands cupping her glass of water. "That makes sense. Things didn't go too well this summer. But these people came to you; this isn't you just 'messing with things you shouldn't.' "

It was Hazel's turn to give Kate a look.

"I'm not trying to get you to teach me!" Kate laughed. "Honest!"

Hazel sighed. "Well, I know I'm not sleeping again unless I look into this."

"Yes!" Kate whispered into her glass, giving Hazel shifty eyes over the brim.

Hazel gave her leg a good-natured shove. The jolt sloshed water down Kate's chin.

"Technically, I did keep my end of the bargain." Kate grinned. "I finished my essay. No all-nighter for me."

"The deal was boxes, too, so I'll see you in the morning." Hazel half rose from her seat.

"No!" Kate laughed, pulling her back down. "I'll unpack, I promise."

Hazel sat back with a grin, but their expressions soon turned serious. Except for the Shadow's chain, Hazel had never truly tried to travel by cord. It was Riley who had visited Hazel. She knew how to feel for the cords with her heart and how to follow them a short distance by eye, but she thought she understood how he did it.

After several calming breaths and a few minutes of sifting through the cords from her heart, Hazel slumped and opened her eyes.

"I can't find anything," she said.

Kate opened one eye and said, "Oh good, I thought it was just me."

"No, but I didn't really expect you to find them. You have no connection to them. I barely do. And that's the problem."

Hazel paused as realization dawned on her. "Riley and I must have been connected because our shadows knew each other."

Kate pursed her lips, nodding as she took this in. "But if these people have no connection, and we know for a fact you have no more Shadow, how did they find you?" she mused.

The two girls sat in silence so long that they both started to yawn.

"Let's visit Riley," Kate suggested at last. "We have a connection to him, and he knows more about this than we do."

Hazel nodded and stifled another yawn. She closed her eyes again and found Riley's cord. She felt the couch cushion shift as Kelly settled in to do the same. Just as she had this summer, Hazel imagined placing her hands on the cord and pulling. This time, she pulled herself forwards instead of pulling Riley towards her. The room blurred around her and it was as if she was pulling herself through the furniture, the wall, through town—buildings and all. She passed long stretches of forest, and, all within seconds, found herself in a darkened bedroom.

Hazel recognized the twin bed and the figure lying atop it. She had been here once before while inside a mirror. She bounced towards the bed, beaming at having managed this feat. She felt Kate's presence over her shoulder but couldn't see her.

"We did it!" she said, but no one heard her. Realizing she would not be able to wake Riley up without being heard, Hazel stretched out a hand to shake him, but her hand passed right through. She pursed her lips. She was about to try speaking again when the sensation of Kate's hand gripped her shoulder a little too tight.

The open closet door had twitched. Hazel's heart lurched. Something was dangling from the ceiling inside and had nudged the door. As she watched, a body descended from a slab in the roof and fell to the floor. It rose to stand in the darkness. There was a man in Riley's closet.

Petrified, Hazel stared as the man crept out, his eyes fixed on Riley's sleeping form. His hair hung around his face in strings, but Hazel couldn't make out the rest of his features. He approached Riley's bed and stood over him. His head tilted as if puzzled.

He either hadn't seen Hazel or couldn't. She remained like a statue, wracking her brain for a way to wake Riley. The man raised a hand over Riley's form and moved it back and forth as if sensing something. Then he turned and swooped down on the piles of clothes all over the floor, tossing them about as he searched. Hazel flinched at the sudden movement but didn't waste another moment. She rushed to Riley's side to shake him awake.

Then the man was back. Hazel froze again, face-to-face over Riley's body. This close, she could see that his black hairline was receding in a widow's peak.

The man licked his thin upper lip and said, "Not yet."

Hazel's breath trembled, but the man wasn't looking at her. He bent over Riley again, and Hazel was pretty sure he didn't know she was there at all.

He held something small to his chest and said, "Pull."

Hazel was wrenched backwards. The man's head snapped up at the sudden change, but Hazel was already gone.

6

Chapter 6: Riley

Riley dropped his ear to the chest of his own sleeping body. He let out a sigh of relief. He was still breathing. He took a step back, gaping, and his heels went through the piles of discarded clothes on his floor. He kicked at them, but nothing shifted. He raced to the hallway to test if his mom could see him in the living room, but the lights were out throughout the house. He must have been asleep longer than he'd thought. He poked his head into her room and found her snoring in peace. Riley let his hands pass through the doorframes on either side of her room instead, then paused.

A light had caught his eye from the right. At the end of the hallway, a new door had appeared. It was a simple door of plain brown wood, matching all the others in the house, but it was ajar. A blue light from within reflected on the hardwood floor.

"Hello?" he called, his footsteps making no noise as he approached the door. His voice echoed the way the blue-eyed girl's voice at the dance had. Was she on the other side again?

Riley reached out a hand to pull the door open. Just when his fingers touched the wood, something dark shifted behind him.

He whirled around.

"Mom?" Riley whispered. "Charlie?"

Fire erupted somewhere between his shoulder blades. Riley was yanked down the hallway as if by a chain. His world went dark and pressed in on him from all sides, compressing his lungs. The pressure on his ears made them pop like he was on an airplane. He couldn't tell where he was, if he was lying on the ground or standing upright. The pressure reached an unbearable pitch, but it went on and on until Riley lost all sense of passing time. He wanted to scream, but the pressure worsened when he tried. His thoughts wouldn't organize beyond all-encompassing terror and pain.

It was over. The floor was freezing against his cheek. Riley scrambled to find his feet, gasping for air. His limbs practically floated after their confinement, and he overbalanced, crashing back to the floor. With shaking hands, he managed to push himself into a sitting position.

As his eyes adjusted to the dark, Riley took in the small room. There was a shabby grey desk and no other furniture. He had never seen this room before. The floor was a grey laminate that mimicked hardwood, and the walls were sage green with no windows. Two unlit strips of fluorescent lights hung over his head.

Riley launched himself at the door, but his hands went through the handle. His palms met solid wood. He banged his fists against it. This didn't make sense. At home his hands had passed through the doorframes. Something was keeping him from leaving.

"Hey!" he cried. "Someone let me out! Hello?"

"I'm so sorry," a voice spoke behind him.

Riley whipped around to see the woman from his nightmare

standing in the corner. He backed into the door, trapped.

"I'm not going to hurt you," she said, and tears sparkled in her eyes. "I've been trying to warn you."

For the first time, Riley could see her features clearly. She had straight, dark hair that settled on her shoulders. She was slim with olive skin, a short nose, and mildly crooked teeth. She wore all black, as if in mourning.

Riley tried the door handle behind him again. The woman didn't move from her corner; she only watched him with a pained expression. Riley's chest was so constricted again he struggled for breath. It was like there was no air in this room with the nightmare woman. What if he couldn't get back to his body?

Footsteps sounded outside the door.

"Help!" Riley screamed, banging on the door again without turning his back. "I'm stuck in here! Please let me out!"

The footsteps stopped on the other side.

"Hurry!" Riley said, his eyes never straying from the woman.

The door swung open, and Riley dodged out of the way, but the man who entered didn't step aside for him. He fixed his eyes on Riley and shut the door again.

"W-what are you doing?" Riley asked. "I need to get out."

"Riley," the man growled, "it's good to meet you."

Riley opened and closed his mouth. He was sure he had never seen this man before. He was a foot taller than Riley with a pallid face and dark circles under his staring eyes. The black hair tucked behind his ears looked unwashed and unkempt. Riley couldn't back away from his unblinking eyes without getting closer to the nightmare woman.

"You killed my kin," the man said through clenched teeth.

"I—I haven't killed anybody," Riley stammered, and he took

a step towards the desk, the only other option.

The man shook his head and a piece of hair fell loose, swinging back and forth in the dark. His lip pulled up in a sneer and he spat, "You ripped my kin to pieces."

It clicked. Riley's insides clenched as his blood froze. He was looking at another shadow.

7

Chapter 7: Kelly

Sixteen Months Ago

Kelly was ready to collapse on her old bed and sleep for the night, but Logan planted his feet on her front lawn.

"We're supposed to go through those doors!" he argued.

"So go through them!" Kelly snapped from the front steps. "What do you need me for?"

Logan's face scrunched in pain. "I can't! I've tried, but I can't. They pull me in, day after day, but I can't pass through. Can't you feel them calling us?"

Kelly pressed her lips together and gazed up at the reddening sky. The truth was, she could. She had felt it even before the library. It was like having a mild thirst, a constant tug at the back of her mind, reminding her where the water waited.

Logan sighed. "I have had to watch all these ghosts soar right by me and pass on so easily, and here I am. Still. I don't even know how long it's been."

She met his eyes and swallowed when she saw the loneliness there. A lump formed in her throat.

"I've had no one to talk to, no one to help me, for … months? Years? And then you finally arrived!" His eyes glistened with hope. "Please. You have to help me leave. I know you're the answer."

Kelly threw up her hands in an exhausted sort of way. "I don't know anything that you don't. We don't even know if I can pass through."

"But I'm sure you can! You just have to try."

She shook her head, ignoring the lump in her throat. "I can't go on yet. I have to know what closed that door. If that thing is what I think it is … I can't ignore it." A small voice in her head added, *this time.* "Goodnight, Logan."

She drifted through the door and left him on the lawn. For a moment she waited on the threshold, but he didn't follow her.

When the covers slid over her at last, the cool pillow caressing her cheek, Kelly burst into tears of relief. Grief and longing for her old life followed hard on its heels, and pierced Kelly's heart so fiercely she curled into a ball to keep from screaming.

Sleep didn't come that night. Hours passed. Kelly fell into a meditative state where she stared at the light fixture on the ceiling, tears drying on her cheeks. She watched the colours changing from black, to grey, to the orange of sunrise. Then she rose and slouched down the stairs, wondering bleakly if she needed food when she didn't have a body.

The fridge was empty. Was it because Hazel had cleaned it out, or because food didn't exist over here? She put a hand to her stomach. She had no desire to eat, no feeling of emptiness, and no thirst parching her throat. She didn't even need to use the toilet after the long, sleepless night. This part of being a ghost had not changed. She sighed, wondering what to do with herself without her little routines.

In the bathroom under the stairs, Kelly turned on the tap to splash water on her face. The second the water touched her skin, it reversed back to the tap like someone had pressed rewind. Her mouth dropped open. She tried a few more times, and her skin crawled when the same thing happened. She looked at her pale face in the mirror. This place was like a fun house version of her own home.

She turned on her heel and ran for the door, bumping straight into Logan on the front step. He caught her arms to stop her from tumbling backwards. He was refreshingly solid. Kelly paused a moment, soaking up the feel of his warm hands on her bare arms. Then she met his eyes and they both took a hasty step back.

"Sorry—" they said at the same time.

Logan gave her a timid smile, stuffing his hands into his pockets. Then, like yesterday, he began chattering, "I'm sorry I pushed you yesterday. It was your first day here and I know I moved too fast. You hadn't even wrapped your head around this place yet. I forgot what it was like when I arrived, and that was selfish of me. I should have given you some time to adjust. I'm really sorry."

He didn't give her a chance to forgive him, but rushed on. "How *was* your first night? I spent my first night running around trying to find *anyone* ... It was so quiet." He shivered. "Then I went back to the school and slept behind a big garbage can because ... well, I don't live here. It was awful. Not that I actually slept."

He paused to look at her, and she realized it was her turn to talk.

"Yeah ... Do we not need sleep here?"

"Isn't it weird?" he said, enthusiasm dripping off him as he leaned towards her.

The corner of Kelly's lip quirked into an involuntary smile.

"And we don't need food or anything either!" he said. "But I still miss it. I would die again for a bite of my mom's four-cheese lasagna."

Kelly didn't know what to say to that. It was obvious that Logan would have had a mother in life, but the thought hadn't occurred to her before now. She wanted to ask how he had died, but that seemed too personal for a one-day acquaintance. She stepped off the front step onto the lawn, but wound up staring at the empty neighbourhood.

"What do you do all day?" she asked.

"I've got some favourite spots," he said. "I like to watch the birds when I'm not flying myself. Actually, there's a cool spot by the mountains I can show you. Come on!"

With that, he stepped into the air and waved for her to follow.

***

Kelly gazed out over the city with her legs dangling off a cliff. Down below was a forest of evergreen trees in a semicircle. The circle created a wind tunnel, and a flock of small black birds was drifting on the currents. The sun was dazzling today, illuminating the red and orange leaves of the deciduous trees that sprinkled the mountain. She could see why this was Logan's favourite spot. At the moment, his eyes were shut and a peaceful smile crossed his face as he soaked in the sunlight.

Kelly located the library in the distance, with its fountain in a patch of water. She could feel it calling her back.

"Why this town?" she asked at last. "This place isn't so special."

Logan opened one eye to study her. "You know this place."

Kelly shifted on the cliff edge. "It's my home."

Logan nodded. "It's not mine."

The birds called to each other down below. Logan was hinting again that Kelly was important to all this.

She swallowed as she watched them dive together. "I'm not that special."

Logan laughed through his nose. "I wouldn't be so sure."

She gave him a disparaging look.

"I tried to leave, you know," he said, nodding into the distance. "I live somewhere that way. Lived. But I couldn't get farther than the mountains. Those doors in the library pulled me back ... The farther I got, the harder it was to move until I couldn't fight against it anymore."

"So we're stuck here," Kelly said.

"Not exactly."

Kelly pressed her lips together. They were back to talking about the doors in the library. Her library.

"I fit here," Kelly said, arching an eyebrow at him. "You don't. Maybe that means you're the special one."

With that, she hopped onto the thin air over the cliff and began climbing down the long imaginary steps to the ground.

"Wait!" Logan cried, hurrying after her. "Where are you going?"

She looked over her shoulder at him, the stranger she had just met.

"To find answers," she said at last.

8

Chapter 8: Hazel

N^{ow} Hazel twisted around, reorienting herself in the darkened living room rather than Riley's bedroom. Her pulse was pounding. Across the couch, Kate was doing the same, her eyes wide and round. Hazel's lips tingled from being away from her body so long.

"Do you think it saw you?" Kate asked. Her hands were clenched on her blanket.

Hazel shook her head. "I don't know."

"There can't be another shadow!" Kate cried. "There just can't be!"

"What?" Hazel asked, her pitch rising. "What shadow?"

"The one at Riley's!" Kate answered. "Didn't you see it?"

"No!" Hazel said, blood draining from her face. "I saw a man. I didn't see any shadow. Are you sure?"

Kate nodded about five times in the space of a second. "That's why I pulled you back! I could feel it in the dark. We have to wake Riley!"

Hazel dove for her phone on the coffee table. She pulled up her contacts and found Riley's number. Hoping that they were wrong and that Riley was about to be woken in the middle of the night for no reason, she dialed.

There was no answer after the first ring. Hazel looked over at Kate, who was leaning in and biting hard on her lower lip. The second ring came and went. Then the third.

"Come on, Riley," she muttered.

"You've reached Riley," the voicemail said.

Hazel hung up before it could get to the recording.

"Are you sure you saw a shadow?" she asked.

"Yes!" Kate insisted. "Only I didn't *see* it. I couldn't see anything. I could feel your presence and Riley's, but someone else was there too, and a shadow. And I had this feeling in my gut, this dark knot, like everything was wrong and you weren't safe."

"Me?" Hazel repeated. "Not Riley?"

Kate shrugged and shook her head in confusion. "Maybe because it's you who I was touching."

"And you pulled me back," Hazel said.

Kate nodded. "I hope I did it in time."

Hazel knew better than to dismiss Kate's feeling of a presence. She knew how valuable gut feelings were. She dialed again. Then again. When she hung up a fourth time, she and Kate shared a worried stare.

"What do we do?" Kate whispered.

Hazel opened and closed her mouth, at a loss.

"Call the police?" Kate suggested.

Hazel raised her phone again, but then stopped. "I don't know his address. And how would I explain?"

Kate shook her head 'I don't know' and said, "It's worth it

though."

So Hazel dialed.

***

An hour later, Hazel's phone rang back. Kate had fallen asleep chewing her nails, and Hazel's head had eventually bobbed until it met the armrest. They both jerked awake at the sound of the ringtone, and Hazel snatched up the phone.

"Hello?"

It was the same 9-1-1 operator Hazel had called earlier. The woman had found Riley's address by contacting his cell phone provider, and the police had gone to check on him.

"His mother let them in and they confirmed that he's safe in bed," the woman said. "So there's nothing to worry about."

Hazel let out a sigh of relief and slumped back onto the couch. "Thank you so much," she said. "I'm so sorry I bothered you with this."

When the call was over, she let her head fall to her other shoulder so she could see Kate. "I guess we were worried over nothing."

Kate wrapped her blanket around her shoulders as if chilled by the thought. "We both know what we saw ..."

Hazel checked the time on her phone and groaned. "I'm not going to be able to keep my eyes open in class." She stood up, ready to head back to bed. "Come on. We've done what we can."

"We should call him in the morning," Kate insisted, standing too. "Just to be sure."

They trudged up the stairs together, Hazel still turning over the night in her mind. They said goodnight on the landing, and crept back into their own beds. Jen was sleeping with a small smile on her lips, but it took Hazel a long time to shake the memory of people encircling her before she could shut her eyes.

***

At the kitchen table the next morning, Hazel and Kate exchanged a glance over their toast. Jen was filling her traveller's mug with coffee by the sink. Riva was not up yet.

"Did you call him?" Kate mouthed.

Hazel mouthed back, "No answer."

"Same here."

Jen sat down between them. She took a sip of her coffee before speaking, as was her way. "How come you're up so early, Kate?"

"Couldn't sleep," Kate said, rising and taking her plate of toast to the living room. Over Jen's shoulder she mouthed, "You should tell her."

Hazel turned back to Jen in time to meet her smile.

"What time will you be back from class today?" Jen asked.

"I've got wrestling after, so not until four-ish. You?"

Jen had a part-time job in a clothing store in the mall, so when she wasn't in class or playing basketball, she was at work.

"Probably five."

Hazel bit her toast, buying herself some time to figure out what to say.

"Did I tell you my mom wants us over for dinner Sunday?" Jen asked.

Hazel smiled. "Your mom always wants us over."

"You know you love her," Jen teased, leaning in to kiss Hazel's forehead. "I got to run. See you tonight."

Hazel finished her toast at the window over the sink as she watched Jen drive away. She waved her off, guilt curling in her gut. She would tell Jen the truth tonight.

Thursday was Hazel's day to walk to school since Jen needed to borrow her car for the longer commute. She left earlier

45

than usual this morning, letting the slow walk in the weak October sun settle her nerves. It had rained in the night, and the pavement sparkled with little puddles reflecting the grey sky. Hazel blew out a stream of cloudy breath and watched the wind snatch it up. When she looked back down, the ghost woman from the driveway was blocking the sidewalk up ahead.

Hazel tapped her necklace with her fingernail so that it made a faint *tink*. She didn't slow her pace. When she was within 30 feet of her, the woman disappeared like Hazel's breath, just a cloud for the lavender to push away. Hazel sighed. She wished she had found this necklace years ago.

9

Chapter 9: Riley

"Please, don't hurt me," Riley said, one hand raised in defence as he backed towards the desk.

The man scoffed. "You deserve it."

Riley's heart beat so fast he could feel it in his fingertips. He glanced over at the woman in the corner. The man's eyes snapped in her direction.

"Sasha!" he shrieked. Riley jumped in alarm. It was like someone else was speaking. "Get out of here, now!"

Sasha backed away through the wall without another word. The man pointed a finger at Riley.

"You stay away from her," he hissed through his teeth.

Riley raised both hands. With the woman gone, he rounded the desk to put space between them. "I will. You got it. I promise."

But the man pursued him around the desk. Riley clenched his fists, trapped between fight and flight. He backed all the way into the corner, and the man stopped with his face inches away. Why couldn't Riley back through the wall like Sasha could?

"I need some answers," the man said.

Riley nodded, ready to tell the man anything he wanted to hear if he would only let him leave.

"Who else do you know that can see ghosts?"

Riley met his cold brown eyes with surprise. "N-no one."

The man growled in rising anger, and Riley flinched, his shoulders rising to his ears.

"I can keep you here," the man said, slamming a closed fist against the wall, "forever. I know all about Travellers like you."

"I don't know anyone," Riley rasped, his mouth too dry. "Ghosts aren't real."

The man chuckled, and Riley did not like it. "That's funny," he said. "You're very funny. Did you forget who we just saw in the corner?"

Riley didn't dare speak. The man raised a hand and tapped a finger to Riley's temple. A jolt of pain shot through Riley's head and radiated down the nerves of his neck like an electrical fire. He gasped in pain.

The man's smile revealed his narrow bottom teeth. "Imagine if I held on longer. You should never have left your body, Traveller-boy."

His body. "I–I have to get back," Riley choked out. The last time he had followed the cords and left his body for too long, he had nearly died.

"You won't be going back."

"But—"

"Your body will be claimed by someone soon enough. In fact, I might go back for it myself." The man looked thoughtful. "I'm sure your friends would let me get nice and close."

Cold rippled down Riley's arms as he thought of this shadow possessing his body. He could be trapped here as someone impersonated him and took over his life. He thought of his mom, of Sophie and Wyatt, and the danger they would be in.

"What did they ever do to you?" Riley whispered.

"It's not what they did to me," the man said, wetting his lips. "Not like with you. It's what they can do *for* me."

Riley frowned. "Why can't I do it? Just tell me what you need."

"I need their names," the man repeated. "All the ghost-seers."

Riley glanced over the man's shoulder to where Sasha had disappeared. "But you can see ghosts yourself. Why do you need them?"

The dark eyes darted back and forth between Riley's. Then he backed off. He continued to study Riley as if thinking about his answer. With one sharp turn he walked out and slammed the door behind him.

Riley sank to the floor behind the desk, his legs like jelly as he let the darkest corner of the room swallow him.

"Just wake up," he muttered to himself. He squeezed his eyes shut as tight as he could, then forced them open.

He was still in the dark room. He leapt to his feet, hoping a burst of adrenaline would do the trick, but still nothing changed. Like a prisoner, he ran his hands in a line along all four walls, returning back to where he started. No matter how hard he pushed, there was no getting through. He spent extra attention on the ghost woman's corner, testing every inch of the two walls. The paint was smooth and cold, and near the bottom it met a thin lip of black plastic that separated it from the faux-wood floor. Riley couldn't get through any of it.

The man had called him a Traveller, not a ghost. There must be some difference between travelling from your body and being separated from it by death. Riley wished he knew the rules. He turned his eyes to the desk. It had three stacked drawers on one side. He tried to yank one open, but his hand came away empty. Evidently the only things he could interact with were the walls and floor. But why?

10

Chapter 10: Kelly

Sixteen Months Ago

Kelly opened the front door before Logan could knock.

"Good morning!" he said, beaming despite the rain soaking his hair and clothes.

Kelly put her hand out to feel the drops splash onto her palm. Until now, every morning had been the same. Logan would knock at the same time every day, and they would head out into the cool October sunshine. How he knew what time it was, Kelly didn't know. Her own sense of time was muddled. The seconds, minutes, and days merged into each other at a speed that was hard to grasp.

She watched the raindrops hit her palm and reverse back into the sky for another try.

"Cool, huh?" Logan said.

When she looked closer, Kelly saw the rain was also reversing off Logan. There was a mist around him where the falling rain and reversing rain collided.

"It's like the weather is rejecting us," she said.

"I keep saying we're not supposed to be here," Logan replied, but he shrugged it off. "Still, it's cool. And if you concentrate, you can make the rain go right through you."

Just like she had when her hand went through the tree, Kelly relaxed her palm and watched the next raindrops slip through. She inspected her hand. It was dry.

"But it's hard to maintain," Logan admitted. "Might as well get wet." He gestured to the road. "Shall we?"

They made their way across the marshy grass, their footprints springing back up as they left the yard for the road. It was like they had never crossed the grass at all.

"Have you seen any doors yet?" Kelly asked.

Logan shook his head. "No, but I did see eight robins on the walk over here. This weather is perfect for worms."

Kelly suppressed an eye roll. They were supposed to be patrolling the city for portals, not birds. So far, they had encountered five doors, all glowing blue, but Kelly had never been fast enough to do more than shout Hazel's name before they closed. Logan assured her she wouldn't be able to get through one anyway, but Kelly was determined to try for herself. She wished he would take it more seriously.

"Before you ask, no, I haven't seen any shadows either," he went on. "But I got to say, it's a lot creepier looking for one in this weather."

They left Kelly's neighbourhood behind. The wind whistled like a ghoul between the buildings, pelting them with rain. Kelly eyed blank window after blank window, imagining the Shadow was peering back. She rolled her shoulders to shake off the feeling.

"So when the zombies finally died—" Logan began, continuing a conversation from yesterday.

"The corrupt," Kelly corrected.

"Right. When the corrupt died, did their souls go through the doors then?"

Kelly shook her head. "No, I don't think so. The Shadow had used them up, eaten them as an energy source."

"That's terrible ..." Logan looked sick at the thought.

"You have no idea," Kelly said, her teeth chattering.

Logan stopped walking and looked up at the hospital on their right. "Maybe we should go inside and warm up," he said. "See if any doors turn up in there."

Grateful for the suggestion, Kelly followed him through a wall. Her mouth fell open when the rain sloughed off her body and clothes, leaving her dry and comfortable on the other side. Logan grinned.

"Better?"

"Much!" Kelly said, running her fingers over the fabric of her dry black t-shirt.

"Dark in here," Logan commented.

Away from the external windows, Kelly felt like an intruder in the cave of a sleeping giant. They tiptoed down the main hall, feeling their way along the walls. Logan pressed a button for one of the elevators lining the hall, but as expected, nothing happened. Kelly shrugged. Hall after hall, they found no unexpected doors. Kelly led the way, remembering some directions from visiting her mom at work.

"I used to think I'd work here someday," Kelly whispered as they looked in on the empty staffroom. Her heart panged with grief over her own lost future.

"I'm sorry," Logan replied.

Kelly shrugged again and continued on. "What did you think you were going to do?"

Logan stuffed his hands in his pockets.

"Why do you look like that?" Kelly asked, a smile creeping up on her face.

"You're going to laugh," he said.

She raised her eyebrows, daring him to try her.

"Ornithology," he admitted. "The study of birds."

Kelly did laugh then. She raised her hands in apology. "That makes perfect sense. I could absolutely see you doing that. It suits you."

He grinned. "I'm glad you think so."

But Kelly's smile slipped off her face as her fingers found the wall to trace it to the next room. "Too bad neither of us will get to do what we dreamed."

Logan caught her other hand before she could walk away. Kelly caught her breath.

"Hey," he said, "we don't know what's next. Maybe we will."

She managed a weak smile, even though she doubted it.

***

They climbed the darkened stairwell to the next floor, but there Kelly paused with her hand on the door to the second floor.

"What is it?" Logan asked.

"If we're looking for death doors," she said, "we should go to the most common places people die."

Logan nodded. "Go on."

"Well, that would probably be the Operating Room in the ER, or the Long-term Care Ward."

"Okay, so which one do you want to try?"

Kelly bit her lip. She had visited Gran upstairs many times, but hadn't been back since the day she died.

"Long-term Care," she said finally, squaring her shoulders.

"It feels a bit wrong, doesn't it?" Logan asked when they rounded another corner to trudge up the next flight. "We're like those tornado chasers. Only we're chasing people's deaths."

"We've got a good reason," Kelly said, her voice terse. She didn't want to argue about the doors again.

"Still," Logan said, "feels grim."

Kelly set her jaw to stop herself from answering.

When they emerged into the Long-term Care Ward, Kelly couldn't stop the chill that ran down her spine. It was so empty. The absence of nurses bustling from room to room, and old folks sitting in the common area calling, "Eh?" when they couldn't hear each other, made her stomach feel hollow.

She followed her feet to Gran's old room, Logan trailing behind her. Inside, the beds were made. Kelly let her finger graze the blankets at the end of Gran's bed as she drifted towards the window. Tears prickling her eyes, she stared without seeing at the quiet city as trails of rain streaked down the glass.

At last, Logan spoke. "This is where it happened, isn't it?"

Kelly knew he was referring to the Shadow, and a surge of anger pumped through her veins. She felt like something was being stolen from her. The Shadow was gone, but it had even poisoned her grief. Gran should have had a peaceful death at a ripe old age. Kelly should have felt a bittersweet loss, comforting herself that Gran had a good long life. She should have been thinking only of Gran and how she missed her. Instead, her chest ached as grief tangled in the Shadow's web, mixed up with rage and injustice. Instead of a tear of grief, a hot tear of anger raced down her cheek.

She brushed the tear aside and cleared her throat. "This is where Gran died," she answered, claiming the room. "Come on, let's keep looking."

They spent most of the day wandering the ward or lounging on the couches in the common area. Logan found a Scrabble board on a bookshelf, and they whiled away some time playing by a window. The hospital grew darker than ever as night stole into the halls.

Logan sighed and stretched, his long arms reaching wide over his head. "I guess no one died today."

"I guess not," Kelly sighed, packing up the game board. "Maybe we should have tried the ER instead."

"Let's walk through on our way out," Logan suggested.

Once again, Kelly trailed a hand along the wall as a guide. When they reached the ER, she shivered. The lines of benches were like crouching monsters lurking in the darkness, their shadows stretching across the moonlit floor. Their footsteps tapping on the linoleum floor were too loud.

"Let's check out Triage before we go," Kelly said, pointing to an inner door.

Logan followed her into another hall filled with beds. Deeper they crept, until the hall opened into a wide room with more beds for critical care.

"It's just beds everywhere," Logan said, sounding uneasy. "No doors."

Kelly nodded to the Operating Room. "One last try."

She pushed her way through double doors to see a bed in the middle of the room. It was tidy and made. Her shoulders slumped.

She rubbed her temples and said, "I've never wished someone would die, but this is so frustrating. I just want to understand this place."

She glanced to her right for Logan's answer, but he wasn't

beside her. When she looked over her shoulder, his figure was hovering in the doorway.

"What's the matter?"

As if in response, Logan backed out of the room, the double doors swinging out of sync as he turned on his heel.

"Logan, wait!" she called, concern drawing her brows.

Kelly's heart beat faster as she realized she was about to be alone in the silent hospital. She hurried after him, spotting his retreating figure just as he threw his shoulder into the exit doors and stepped out into the rain.

As Kelly passed the rows of benches, a Shadow shifted in her peripheral vision. She froze, adrenaline tingling in her fingertips. The Shadow was here. Had it noticed her, or was it haunting the hospital tonight, much as she and Logan had today? She lingered on the balls of her feet, eyes swivelling around the room. Everything in her screamed for her to run. She fought against it for a moment longer, reminding herself that she never wanted to be that scared little girl again.

But as she teetered on the edge of her decision, she thought of Logan. She couldn't ignore that something had seriously upset him. At last, she tiptoed after him, equal parts disappointment and relief mixing in her stomach.

Logan was speeding down the street, his straight arms pumping. Kelly had to run to catch up to him, rain drenching her in the space of a minute. She grabbed his shoulder, and he gasped like she'd attacked him as he whirled around.

She raised her palms to show she meant no harm. "Logan, what is it?"

"I–I don't know," he stammered, tormented eyes flicking back to the hospital as raindrops ran down his face. "I just ..." He trailed off with a shake of his head and continued walking.

Kelly jogged after him. "Did you sense the Shadow in there?"

"No. Nothing like that."

"Then what?" she insisted, grabbing his shoulder to stop him again.

Logan obliged, but he shifted on his feet like he was barely able to restrain himself. "There was ... something familiar about that room. I can't explain it. Can we get out of here?"

Kelly nodded. Together, they climbed the steps into the air. At that speed, it was minutes before they reached Kelly's house. For the first time, she invited him in.

"I don't know," he said, "I should probably go home."

Kelly had never been to Logan's chosen home either. Being so close to the Shadow today, it suddenly occurred to her that she could wake up alone here tomorrow. The thought made her colder than the rain. She looked sideways at him.

"I don't think I'd want to be alone right now."

He hovered on the lawn, swaying back and forth for a moment, then nodded.

Kelly smiled and led him inside. He followed her into the entrance hall at the bottom of the stairs, and she showed him the kitchen on the right and the living room down the hall.

"The TV doesn't work," she said with an apologetic shoulder raise as they settled on opposite ends of the couch.

"Nothing electronic does," he replied.

After a moment of silence, she broached the topic again. "What happened back there?"

Logan studied the lined pattern in the couch cushions, his fingers tracing the seam. He didn't answer.

In a softer voice, Kelly pressed on. "Logan, how did you die?"

His jaw tensed. His eyebrows drew together and she read the answer there.

"You don't remember?"

He swallowed. "I—I remember feeling ... pain. So much pain. And my hands were warm. From my own blood. The air was steaming from it. In the car. And I felt ... terrified. And I could hear ... I can still hear ... my mom screaming. Screaming over me."

He stopped to rub the back of his neck as if the memory had raised the little hairs there. Kelly clasped her hands together to stop herself from taking his.

"We both knew I was going to die. We must have ended up in the hospital," he went on, "but I don't remember that. I just remember the screaming and the ... fear."

Kelly nodded. "I remember it too."

They locked eyes, understanding passing between them. Then Kelly dropped his gaze. They had experienced the worst, they had died, yet here they were. Here *she* was, prolonging their deaths. It was no wonder Logan was impatient to go on, to put his past behind him.

"Was your mom okay?" she asked after a moment.

"I don't know," Logan sighed. "I think she lived. But the way she screamed ..."

He lapsed into silence, staring into the distance, and Kelly understood. He was worried his mom would never recover from losing her son. Sadness ached in her chest, reminding her of her own mother and grandmother. At least they hadn't witnessed Kelly's death.

Kelly wet her lips and forged on. "This must be why you're stuck here. In this town, not your own. You died here."

Logan didn't answer.

Finally, she said, "Look, let's take our minds off it. I've got games." She stood to open the hallway closet, but Logan rose too.

"I think I'll go home," he said. "Thanks anyway."

He strode past her and out into the night, leaving Kelly with nothing but the falling rain to break the silence.

<h1 style="text-align:center">11</h1>

Chapter 11: Hazel

Every break she got that day, Hazel stepped out of her classrooms to call Riley. Every time she did, the phone rang and rang. Her unease grew. She had asked him for space from the ghost stuff, she reasoned as her classmates filed back into the room. Maybe he had taken it personally. Maybe he was ignoring her, and physically he was perfectly safe.

But as she took her seat, the image of the man dropping from Riley's closet ceiling made her go cold all over again. Kate had said she sensed a shadow. Hazel couldn't see how Riley could be safe, even if his mom had confirmed he was with the police. She had to do something.

"Hazel!" Savannah said, waving a hand in front of Hazel's face.

Hazel blinked. She had somehow made it through the day and now she was sitting on a bench in the weight room, dumbbells at her feet. Wrestling practice consisted of weight training today.

"Sorry, what?" Hazel asked.

"You have to actually lift the weights," Savannah teased,

miming raising the dumbbells up and down.

"Right," Hazel agreed, scooping them up.

"Why are you so distracted today?" Savannah asked, picking out her own weights and sitting on the opposite bench.

Hazel counted out her reps, watching the weight rise and lower in the mirror before answering. "I'm worried about a friend. He's not answering my calls. It's not like him."

"Oh," Savannah grunted as she worked her own weights. "Do you think he's mad at you?"

Hazel shook her head. "I'm worried it's worse than that."

"Oh. Can you drop by?"

Hazel huffed out a little laugh. "He lives really far away."

"Oh," she said again. "That sucks."

"Tell me about it." Hazel sighed. "I don't know what else to do."

"Well, if I was that worried, I'd call his mom." Savannah set her weights down with a thud.

"Don't know her number," Hazel grunted, lifting again.

Savannah rolled her eyes. "You can always find their moms. Haven't you seen those clips of internet trolls getting their moms called on them? You just have to do some digging."

Hazel inclined her head, intrigued. "Think that will work?"

Savannah's eyes twinkled. "I may have done it before."

***

After practice, the two girls dropped into the library to borrow one of the school computers. Hazel logged Savannah into her accounts, and used her own phone to scroll through Riley's socials. Riley went by @RileyE on all his accounts, so there was no surname to go on, and Hazel had never thought to ask. Eventually, however, she found a photo of Riley with two kids who looked younger than him. In the comments, someone had written, "They look so alike!"

"I think I found a family photo," Hazel said.

Savannah swivelled to see it. "Click who commented on that."

Hazel did, but the account was private.

"That's okay," Savannah said. "We got a last name."

Savannah pulled up LinkedIn on the computer and punched in the last name plus Riley's hometown.

"We got a match," she said triumphantly.

"Elisabeth Bricker," Hazel read. "But look at the date here, she hasn't been on to update this in years."

"It's worth a shot," Savannah said.

So, armpits prickling with nervous sweat, Hazel called the company.

"I'm sorry, Elisabeth hasn't worked here in about six years."

Hazel was not surprised. "Do you know where I can reach her?"

"I'm afraid I can't give out that information," the receptionist said.

Hazel grimaced at Savannah as she hung up, but Savannah pointed at the computer screen. While Hazel was on the phone, she had taken to Google to search for Elisabeth Bricker.

"I found this," she said. Her mouth twisted in a grimace.

It was an article announcing the death of Riley's father. Hazel covered her mouth in shock. It was one thing to hear about Liam's death from Riley, it was another to stumble upon it online. Her stomach twisted with guilt at this intrusion, but she couldn't help reading it word for word. Two gang members had attacked Liam while he was hiking the trail behind his home. Liam's photo headed the article. He was smiling a charming, crooked smile that suggested a playful nature. He had the same features as Riley, from nose to cheekbones. The tragedy was that Liam had had the bad luck to cross these men's path. They had been expecting someone else.

"Look here," Savannah said, tapping the bottom of the screen and making Hazel cringe. She hated when people did that.

" 'In lieu of flowers,' " Hazel read, " 'please consider making a donation of any size to support the Brickers' Hobby Farm, which was Liam's passion.' "

"So let's see if we can find this farm," Savannah said, typing in the name.

A few clicks later and they were looking at a picture of a happy family of three standing in front of a cornfield. Liam had his arm over a younger Riley's shoulders, and his other around Elisabeth's waist. Riley was leaning away as if embarrassed, but his smile was genuine. Hazel's heart ached to see him so happy.

"And there you have it," Savannah said, tapping the screen again. She sat back and crossed her arms with satisfaction. There was a 'contact us' section with a phone number.

Hazel clapped Savannah on the back. "Nice one."

***

The girls parted ways as Savannah headed to another class and Hazel headed home. Hazel pulled up her hood against the rain and held the phone under its protection as she crossed the parking lot.

It rang three times before a woman's voice answered. "Hello?"

"Hi. Is this Riley's mom? It's Hazel Connors calling."

"Oh!" Elisabeth said, surprised. "Yes, hi, Hazel."

Hazel cut right to the chase, her voice sounding weird in her ears because of the hood. "I'm calling because I'm wor-

64

ried about Riley. I've called him a few times and he hasn't answered—"

"Yes, he's sleeping," Elisabeth reassured her. "He's been having a lot of insomnia lately, and I think he's finally catching up."

"That's good," Hazel said, distracted as she watched for traffic and splashed across the road. "But the thing is ... I sort of had a–a vision of him."

"A vision," Elisabeth repeated.

"Kind of," Hazel went as she reached the safety of the other side. She turned down a street filled with apartment complexes and dorms. She had to lower her voice as a group of students passed her on the sidewalk. "I saw him sleeping in bed, but then a man came down out of his closet. Like he was in the ceiling."

There was a long pause on Elisabeth's end.

"My worry," Hazel went on, "is that it was another shadow."

More silence.

"E-Elisabeth?"

"The only thing in our attic is raccoons," Elisabeth said at last. "We get them every year."

Hazel wiped her nose, which was beginning to run in the cold. "Are you sure?"

Elisabeth's voice dropped to a comforting whisper. "I'm in his room now. He's still sleeping, safe and sound." Then Elisabeth gasped.

"What is it?" Hazel clutched her phone to her ear.

"The panel to the attic is open."

Hazel stopped walking. She could hear Elisabeth's quickened breathing on the other side.

"I'll get a chair," she whispered at last.

"No!" Hazel almost shouted. "You can't go up there. Not alone!"

The line was quiet again. Then Elisabeth said in a tight voice, "There's no one here to do it for me."

"Maybe the police—" Hazel suggested.

"There's a stool in the hall closet," Elisabeth said at the same time. Then— "Wait. Did you call the police last night?"

Hazel hesitated long enough to confirm. "I didn't have your number," she admitted as Elisabeth let out a long breath of strained patience, "and I was worried."

There was the squealing sound of a closet door on tracks, then some rustling. "Got the stool. I'm going to put you on speaker because I need the flashlight app. But stay quiet so we don't wake Riley."

"Okay," Hazel agreed. She started walking again, dodging a puddle the size of the sidewalk.

Elisabeth groaned as if pulling her upper body into the attic. Then all Hazel could hear was the rain beating against her hood. Finally, another gasp.

Hazel almost dropped her phone. She clutched it to her ear with two hands.

"What is it?"

"There's a bed up there," Elisabeth whispered, her tone high-pitched, "and garbage."

Hazel went cold.

"Is someone up here?" Elisabeth called.

Hazel was walking so fast now she was almost running. A horn blared as she stepped off the sidewalk onto a new road.

Elisabeth swore.

Hazel jerked back, the driver of the passing car glaring at her. She raised her hand in apology as he drove on.

"Elisabeth, are you okay?" Hazel squeaked into the phone, crossing the road at a run.

"What was *that*?" Elisabeth demanded.

"I'm so sorry," Hazel said. "It was a car. I'm walking home from class."

"Scared the life out of me," Elisabeth said, still whispering. "I'm down now, and the panel is shut. But someone was up there."

"What are you going to do?"

"We're getting out of here. Then I'm going to call the police."

"Good," Hazel sighed.

She heard Elisabeth set the phone down with a gentle thud. "Riley, sweetheart, I need you to wake up."

Hazel waited to hear Riley's voice, but it didn't come.

"Riley? Riley, wake up, honey. Riley!"

Hazel couldn't help herself. "Is he okay?"

"He's not waking up," Elisabeth called, and Hazel could hear the hint of panic in her voice.

"He's breathing though, right?" she asked, swiping loose strands of wet hair back from her face.

After a moment, Elisabeth sighed, "Yes."

Hazel shut her eyes for a second. "What are you going to do?"

"I–I'll call the police. And maybe ... the nurse hotline."

"Good," Hazel said, nodding though Elisabeth couldn't see her. "Good idea. I'll hang up. But please call me back."

"Wait."

Hazel waited, her ears ringing with the silence.

"Is there another shadow?"

"I don't know," Hazel admitted.

"But if there is," Elisabeth went on, dread dripping from her voice, "what do I do?"

Hazel chewed her lip. There wasn't much Elisabeth could do to protect Riley from a shadow. A ghost, on the other hand … If they keep the shadow's favourite food far away from Riley, hopefully it would lose interest in him.

"Riley said he ordered a necklace recently," Hazel told her. "The pendant looks like a little jar, and there should be lavender in it. Is he wearing it?"

"No, I don't see one. But he did get something in the mail, hold on."

She could hear Elisabeth rummaging around in the room. "Here's the box. But there's nothing in it."

Hazel groaned. "Okay, lavender then. You can burn it or surround him with it. It helps keep ghosts away."

Elisabeth caught her breath. "Keep ghosts away? Why would we want that?"

"Well—well, for peace of mind," Hazel said, surprised by Elisabeth's tone.

"But ghosts are good," Elisabeth insisted. "We want ghosts. How do we get rid of shadows?"

"Well, I—I only know the difficult way … and Riley's obviously not up for that right now …"

"Then I have to go," Elisabeth said. "I have to call the police." She hung up.

Hazel stared at her phone for a second, watching raindrops splatter on the screen before tucking it into her pocket. She jogged the rest of the way home in an attempt to chase away her nerves.

12

Chapter 12: Riley

The morning sun struggled to trickle into the office room from under the closed door. The growing light was so slight, Riley didn't notice it at first. But there was nothing else to notice. No one entered the building as the morning went on. No one drove by outside. There was only Riley.

Exhausted as he was, Riley finally slept. He passed out with his back against the far wall and his head nodding. At last, the woman didn't bother him, and he entered a state of blank unawareness. When he woke up again, he ran his hands through his hair ruefully. Now he needed her to visit. She, at least, might have some answers.

"Sasha?" he whispered.

There was no response. No one knew better than Riley that a ghost didn't come just because you called. His dad never had. Riley chewed the inside of his cheek, determined to think of something. He closed his eyes and reached for his cords. He should be connected to Sasha.

To his surprise, the colours had changed. Most of the cords

had turned a dull, dead grey that made Riley's stomach uneasy. The others were an electric purple he had never seen before. With his mind's eye, Riley reached out a hand and stroked one of the purple cords. The whole line vibrated, leaving a blur of light in his eyes. When it had settled, Riley reached for one of the grey ones, but his hand passed right through.

He pictured Sasha, and one of the purple cords lit up brighter than the others. He sent a mental message down the line, "Please ... come back. Tell me what's going on."

He opened his eyes as if she would appear in front of him, but the room was as empty as ever. Then her voice echoed in his chest.

"Don't use your cords. I'll come when I can."

He pressed his luck. "Why can't you come now?"

"He's awake" was all she said.

"Who is he?" Riley asked.

When his question was met with silence, Riley rested his head against the wall again, a lump of frustration and disappointment in his throat. Then the fear returned. What if his mom was in danger? He tried to call up her cord, but all that happened was one of the grey cords glowed a little, then went out. He tried to grasp it, but his hands fell through again. He felt for Hazel's, but it too was grey.

With nothing else to do, he got up and started pacing. Why was he blocked from the people who could help him? Riley had never encountered a shadow so powerful.

***

Hours later, when he had the room memorized by steps and turns and had gone back to sleep, a voice said, "Riley, wake up."

For a moment Riley thought it was his mom, but then he

remembered where he was. His eyes flew open and he flinched back. He registered the straight, black hair first.

"It's me," Sasha said. "You're okay."

Riley sat up straight, narrowing his eyes. "Am I?"

"Yes," she said, bowing her head as if ashamed of herself. "I really tried to warn you. It was hard to get away from him though. And I've never visited someone in their dream before. It was hard to maintain. I'm sort of new to this death thing."

When she met his eyes, Riley saw sincerity there.

"How do I get out of here?" he asked.

Her eyebrows inclined even higher in the middle. She raised her shoulders in a gesture of helplessness. "I don't know. You're essentially a living ghost, but the shadow has worked out a way to contain you with its chains. They're tethered to this room, wrapped around it so you can't leave."

"But you can," Riley pointed out. "How are you doing it?"

She said simply, "They're not for me."

Riley ran his hands over his face. "So what am I supposed to do then?"

"One thing I do know," Sasha said, "is you can't use your cords. That's what he wants. He consumes ghosts, and any ghost you reach out to, he can find. You have to keep them safe."

"But he doesn't consume you," Riley persisted.

Sasha looked down again, her lips turning into a straight line for a moment. "He loves me."

Riley's eyes widened in disbelief.

"Ray is my husband," Sasha explained.

"Excuse me?"

"I know," she said. "I know. But you have to understand, when I died, he ... he fell apart. It was an accident. But he felt so guilty. He couldn't let me leave, and then the shadow found us … And he made a deal."

Riley frowned. "What do you mean, he made a deal?"

"He would feed the shadow as long as he could keep me." Her eyes were imploring, begging Riley to understand. "It was to protect me."

"But … what is he feeding it?"

There was a shimmer in Sasha's eyes as she forced herself to say, "Ghosts. The ghosts who come to him."

Riley waved his palms. "Wait, wait, wait. Your husband can see ghosts?"

Sasha nodded, her hair swinging over her shoulders in the dark. "It's why the shadow chose him."

Riley tugged at the shirt he had so carefully chosen yesterday. It was hopelessly wrinkled as his body back home continued to sleep in it. He shivered. He knew what it was like to be chosen by a shadow.

"But it needs you now," Sasha went on. "Word has spread among the ghosts that they have to avoid Ray. And if he doesn't feed it more, eventually it will break the deal and take me."

Riley met her eyes again and realized what his capture meant for her. There was no happy resolution here.

"If I bring ghosts here, they'll be taken."

Sasha swallowed. "Yes."

"But if I don't, you'll be taken."

"Yes."

Riley hung his head in sympathetic misery. "That's brave of you then. To tell me not to."

"I never wanted this," Sasha whispered.

"And you can't talk to him because the shadow is always listening," Riley mused.

Sasha nodded. "Sometimes I can slip away when he's asleep. If they're both asleep."

"And you can't just leave?"

Sasha opened and closed her mouth. Riley knew she was conflicted about leaving her husband in his possessed state. "If I really wanted to ... I'd need a door."

Riley's mind flew to the door he had seen in the hallway outside his bedroom.

"I–I've seen a door," he said.

Sasha smiled. "Of course you have. You're a Traveller."

Riley frowned. "He called me that. Your husband."

"Well, yes," Sasha agreed. Then her face froze with fear. She vanished.

Riley jumped to his feet. "Sasha?"

His voice echoed in the silent office. He turned in a circle, but he was alone. The shadow, or maybe her husband, must have woken up. Riley paced the office with one hand trailing on the walls. Now that he knew what to look for, he could sense the chains Sasha spoke of encircling the room. Claustrophobia tightened his throat. He returned to the door and set about banging his fists against it again.

"Help!" he cried, praying someone would hear him. "Someone! Help me!"

After an hour, his fists were as sore as if he really were hitting his body against the door. He sunk to the ground, leaning against the wooden surface. He might as well be shouting into a different world for all the response he got. Riley supposed this was what it was like for ghosts until they found someone like him. Maybe if Hazel were here, she could hear him.

"Ah," he said aloud. "That's why he wants to know about other mediums."

The shadow needed more ghost-seers so it could find more ghosts. Which meant Hazel was in danger too.

There was a distant creaking sound. Riley sat upright. There was a long stretch of silence, and then footsteps. He scurried away from the door, wondering if he should scream for help or hide. The footsteps came closer. They stopped outside his door. Riley waited, hardly breathing. Keys jingled in the lock, and the door swung open.

A man in a blue uniform peered inside. Riley's eyes widened with hope.

"Sir!" he cried. "You have to help me!"

The security guard scanned the room, oblivious to Riley's presence. He backed away, pulling the door with him.

"No!" Riley cried.

He threw himself at the crack in the door, but the chains caught him around the middle. The door began to slide through him. He reached his hand under the chain, forcing past an invisible barrier. Straining with all his might, Riley grabbed the guard's leg. His hand went through it, and the door closed, leaving Riley squarely where he had started.

"*Brr*," the guard shivered on the other side. Then his footsteps continued down the hall.

"No!" Riley cried again. "Come back! Please!"

His efforts were wasted.

13

Chapter 13: Kelly

N^{ow} Kelly stomped her foot in the slow-moving river in the deserted, hilly park. She was furious with herself, and with Logan. The water splashed into the air, then settled back down again like someone had pressed rewind on the TV.

Logan had been right about time being different in the next layer. She had the strange sense that every day that had passed, every moment, was the present. Her memories of the time spent in the afterlife were as easy to call up as if they had just happened. Yet she must have been here for more than a year.

In that time, her reluctant friendship with Logan had stalled. At first, he had returned to her house every morning, always knocking despite being able to walk through walls. As Kelly traversed the town searching for portals and shadows, Logan had gone from patient to pleading to angry that Kelly wouldn't return to the library. She had been avoiding it since the day the door slammed.

Kelly dropped to the grass at the edge of the river. The autumn leaves rustled around her in the wind, never changing with the seasons. Her heart ached for winter snow, for Christmas movies and curling up under blankets with Hazel and their mom. She imagined Gran arriving with her signature baked peppermint cake and the customary blue laundry basket full of presents under her arm. Kelly hugged her knees.

Her heart panged again when she remembered Gran would inevitably have bought her a book. What she wouldn't give for something to read right now, to cut out some of the loneliness. Even now she felt the call to enter the library, to visit the two doors. Fear clutched her heart. She couldn't. She sprang to her feet and hurried away, walking down the middle of the empty streets.

They had reached a grudging truce since Logan had last stormed off. But Kelly was no closer to discovering what was going on here. The weight of his disappointment and enduring hope sent a knife of guilt through her heart. What was she gaining by staying here? An eternity of loneliness and ostracization from the one person she could talk to?

Eventually her feet found the school, another place that should have been teeming with people. Kelly walked through the gym wall and picked up a basketball off the floor. It had been there since she and Logan had squared off on a happier day. A smile quirked the corner of her lip as she remembered the sound of their laughter and squeaking shoes echoing off the high ceiling. Then the smile slipped away.

She took a few shots to distract herself, the ball swishing through the basket. Then she heard a whisp of thumping music. Kelly whipped around, arms still raised as the ball hit the floor and bounced away. The gym remained dark and empty. Kelly stayed frozen, listening to the silence.

The music came back, like someone was turning the volume up and down. A gust of cold air made her shiver, and her eyes caught on one of the exit doors. They were wide open. Goosebumps sprouting across her arms, Kelly crept towards the doors. Her eyes popped when she saw what was on the other side. Stars were out and shadows bathed the sidewalk. It was *nighttime.* And there were *people.*

"Hello?" she called.

The music got louder. Then she saw the shimmer, the blue water streaming down the doorway. This was not just any door. It was a death door. A soul was about to pass through. Kelly's heart took off racing.

"Hazel?" she called, her voice shaking with hope.

The door was staying open longer than any she had ever seen before. She could see a parking lot beyond the sidewalk, unlike the lawn she was used to. She was afraid if she moved too suddenly, it would vanish like all the other portals.

"Hazel!"

A boy stepped in front of the door, staring straight at her. Kelly froze, pierced through by the sensation of being seen.

"Hey!" she greeted him at last.

She rushed forwards then. Her heart leapt at the prospect of crossing back over to the living world, at leaving behind this constant lonely October. Then pain ripped across her face. She gasped and clutched her nose. Blood ran towards her lip. She had hit some kind of surface.

"Oh!" the boy cried aloud, moving closer as if to help.

Kelly held out a hand to stop him. "I'm fine."

Pinching her smarting nose, she pressed the other hand to the water. Her palm met what felt like a glass shower door, water running down its surface. It was solid yet with a bit of give, and it rippled at her touch. She looked up at the boy. He raised his own hand, but Kelly blinked and he was gone.

"Wait!" she said aloud.

The blue light went out, and she was submerged in darkness. In front of her stood the closed metal exit doors. She ran her hands over them, hoping to feel the water, but the doors were solid and dry. Cautiously, she pushed through it as a ghost. Outside, the wind swirled the leaves on the sunlit pavement.

Disappointment hit Kelly so hard it was like a physical force that knocked her a step back. Her breath hitched and her hands dropped to her sides.

"Why?" she whispered. Her sore nose tingled as tears gathered in her eyes.

So this was it. She couldn't get back through the doors after all. Logan had been right: This was all just a waste of time. She would never see Hazel again.

Kelly forced her feet towards home, tears spilling down her cheeks. They grew hot with her anger, and she brushed them away. When she had come to this place, she had said goodbye to Hazel. It was illogical now to feel the grief hollowing out her stomach as if she hadn't known this was a possibility.

Kelly broke into a run. Even the wind tossing back her hair reminded Kelly of Hazel and how they used to race as kids. Hazel's face had always lit up with determination and joy, and Kelly had ended up sulking when beaten. A laugh bubbled out of her throat, then the tears came in earnest. But why hide them when no one was around to see? Logan was usually at his lookout spot this time of day. She threw back her head and released a scream that echoed off the streets. She heard her own loss, frustration, and loneliness bounce back to her. Somehow, it helped to think of her echo as someone else, as if the pain belonged to someone else.

She didn't bother going up to her room. Neither Jolene nor Hazel was coming home. This was her house now. Kelly threw herself face down on the couch and began beating the cushions as she screamed into the fabric.

She didn't notice when she finally stopped and slipped into stillness and thoughts of family. She turned over and stared at the ceiling. What would her mom say in this moment? Jolene would probably just give her a hug, and Kelly would feel better. She wrapped her arms around herself, knowing it would never be the same. But she would have to be her own parent from now on. It was time to take comfort from her own counsel.

This was going to be hard, but she supposed in the living world, people did it all the time. People grew up and began relying on themselves. They had no idea how lucky they were to have friends and family to encourage them on the path to self-reliance. But for Kelly, the loneliness would never end.

"What do I do now?" she asked the ceiling as a tear ran down her temple.

She could see two options: keep trying to catch a Shadow she had no idea how to stop, or go to the library and pick a door. Either way, it was probably the end. Again.

"Kelly?" Logan's voice called from outside, making Kelly jump.

She debated ignoring him but he continued knocking and calling her name. He sounded worried. Maybe he had seen the Shadow.

Kelly wiped her eyes and rose from the couch. "I'm coming," she called, trying to force her voice to sound normal.

Logan was waiting on the doorstep as usual, his brows pinched with concern. He gasped when he saw her face.

"What?" she asked defensively.

His hand rose as if to cup her cheek, his thumb hovering an inch before her upper lip. Kelly stopped breathing.

"You're bleeding," he said, eyes flicking to hers.

"Oh." Kelly let out a shaky laugh. "I'm fine. Just ... ran into a door."

Logan seemed to realize how close he was standing. He took a step back and let his hand drop. He frowned at her answer. "I was up at my lookout spot, and you didn't walk through the park like you always do. Then I saw you running home and there was this shadowy man following you. I thought he was chasing you."

Kelly's eyebrows flew up in a mixture of surprise and alarm. She hadn't realized Logan knew her so well. But if the Shadow was stalking her, she had bigger concerns. Logan glanced over his shoulder as if the Shadow might be racing towards them even now.

Kelly swallowed. "Well, I guess something was a bit wrong," she admitted. "I found a *door* door. And I couldn't get through it." She indicated to her nose.

Logan's lips parted as he took in all that this meant. Kelly waited for an 'I told you so,' but instead he said, "Oh. I'm sorry."

She pressed her lips into a grim line and nodded her thanks. "Was there really a Shadow?"

Logan nodded. "I'm sure of it. It was so ..." He trailed off and shivered.

"Sounds like the Shadow," Kelly agreed. Her eyes scanned the yard and the houses across the way. "Let's go inside."

Logan followed her in and settled in the living room while Kelly cleaned up her face. When she sat down at the opposite end of the couch, she watched his eyes dart about the space as if the Shadow might be lurking somewhere.

"I don't think it's here," Kelly said, but her hands clenched with nerves.

"*We* aren't supposed to be here," Logan said, his eyes imploring. "Maybe this is what comes after you when you refuse to move on."

Kelly chuckled, trying to be patient. "No, the Shadow I know was on the other side. So it can't be about making us move on if they live over there too."

"But they kill over there," Logan reasoned. "So maybe it *is* about death."

Kelly ran her palms over her eyes for a moment, exasperated. "You're so desperate for it to be about moving on. You don't know the Shadow. It's *evil*. It steals souls *before* they can move on. If it's after me, it's not because it wants to scare me into moving on for my own good." She laughed again. "It's not a helpful being."

Logan was still frowning. "But if it gets us ... we can never move on, right? If it gets us, we're just gone?"

The mirth died on Kelly's face. "I don't know. But I think so."

Logan shifted closer to her on the couch. "So we have to go then. Now, before it's too late!"

Kelly got up with a sigh and paced to the TV and back. It did sound nice to get out of here, wherever that meant. But then the Shadow could hunt some other unsuspecting soul trying to make their way through. Then again, what was she supposed to do about it?

14

Chapter 14: Hazel

Riva had invited Hazel home for dinner to see her family, but Hazel had declined, and Riva had left with a disappointed droop to her shoulders. Meanwhile, Kate was busy working her part-time job at the grocery store. It was the perfect opportunity to speak with Jen.

With a simple meal of pasta in front of them, Hazel took a deep breath and broached the topic.

"I have to tell you something," she began.

Jen raised a wary eyebrow. "Oh?"

Hazel poked at her pasta and said, "I think something—"

Her phone rang. Hazel snatched it up and saw an unknown number. She knew it would be Elisabeth. She answered before it could ring again.

"How did it go?" she asked without preamble. "Are you two okay?"

"I need to know everything about shadows," Elisabeth said, ignoring Hazel's questions. "Is there anything you and Riley might have left out?"

Hazel blinked. "I—I don't think so. I think you know

everything we do.”

"How sure are you the shadow that possessed Riley is dead?"

"Very sure."

"So the shadow in your vision is a new one?"

Hazel rose to her feet, her chair scraping back as she began pacing the kitchen. "I think so. Both our shadows are dead."

"Have you ever heard of a shadow putting someone into a coma?"

Hazel froze inside and out. "Is Riley in a coma?"

Jen whipped around in her chair, lavender hair whirling, to stare at Hazel with wide eyes.

"That's what they're telling me," Elisabeth said, and Hazel could hear the fear through her exhaustion. There was a machine beeping in the background, and Hazel let it reassure her that they were out of the house. "They can't tell me why. Hazel ... it has to be this shadow."

Hazel rubbed her forehead. "But I've never heard of a shadow doing this to someone before. Unless ..."

She stared at the kitchen counter without seeing it. Gran had spent years in the hospital, growing weaker before her time.

"Unless what?" Elisabeth demanded.

"They can attach to regular people and slowly leach their energy, or life, or whatever. But Riley isn't a regular person. And this all happened way too fast."

"Okay, okay," Elisabeth said. "Let's just assume that's what's happening here. What do I do to save him?"

Hazel exhaled a helpless breath and said in a small voice, "I don't know."

"Think harder," Elisabeth insisted, an edge to her voice.

Hazel paced, the silence growing. Finally she said, "Try the lavender. Shadows want ghosts; they're much faster to consume. If it's after Riley, theoretically it should be because he's a ghost magnet. No ghosts, no reason to be interested."

"And you think that will work?"

Hazel pinched her lower lip with her fingers, thinking. "It's the only thing I can think of."

After she hung up, she made eye contact with Jen, whose eyes were as wide as an owl's now.

"So the no-supernatural plan isn't working out, I see."

Hazel dropped into the chair beside her. "I was about to tell you."

Jen sighed and set down her fork. "What's going on with Riley?"

As Hazel explained everything, including the people around their bed, Jen's fingers worried the scars on her neck. But the next words out of her mouth were "Should we go see him?"

For a moment, all Hazel could do was stare as her heart seemed to grow too big for her chest. A wave of warmth swept over her whole body. She couldn't think of the words to express how she felt about Jen in that moment, so she shook her head in wonder and let her eyes do the talking.

Jen blushed, caught off guard by Hazel's sudden change in expression. Then she smiled as if to say, 'What did you expect?' She squeezed Hazel's hand, and Hazel squeezed back.

***

Much like the first time they had met Riley and his shadow, Jen was in favour of holding a group meeting. Unfortunately, Riva was spending the night at her family's, and Kate was working late. It was too short notice for Morgan and Di unless they wanted to video call in again. So Hazel left messages for everyone that they needed to meet tomorrow evening. She figured that would give Elisabeth's lavender a chance to work anyway. If they were lucky, this shadow might leave of its own accord, starve without food, and die.

Hazel and Jen went about their evening, reading their texts or working on assignments, and finally settled under a soft blanket to watch TV. When Kate got home at 10, she dropped her things at the front door and bolted over to Hazel.

"What's happened?"

Hazel paused the TV. "Nothing. Why, what's the matter?"

"You haven't done anything since your message?"

"No."

Kate sighed and collapsed onto the couch. "Oh good."

"That's some twisted FOMO," Jen said with a laugh.

"It's not about missing out," Kate said. "I just don't want Hazel visiting Riley again. Not with cords anyway."

"Oh," Hazel hedged.

Kate read her 'oh' for what it was. "You can't! What if another shadow latches onto you? And this one did something to Riley, something you haven't seen before. Riley needs you. We can't fight these shadows without you!"

Hazel was rather touched, even if she disagreed. "Kate," she said, keeping her tone level, "It's always been 'learn as you go' with these things, and so far it's worked out."

"But—"

"As much as I want to add to Kate's point," Jen interrupted, "we set a meeting for tomorrow. I think we all just need to relax and try not to think about it for now."

Hazel and Kate both opened their mouths, but Jen got there first. She gave Hazel a stern look. "And not doing anything about it, either."

Hazel muttered her grudging agreement as Kate smirked. Kate scooped up her things and went to put them away as Jen turned the TV back on. Hazel tried to concentrate on the show, but she couldn't stop worrying about Riley. When she plugged her phone in that night, she wished it would ring with an update from Elisabeth. She supposed no update meant Riley was still unconscious and nothing worse had happened. She wandered over to the window and pulled back the curtain, careful not to jostle the urns on the ledge.

A dark figure was looking up at her from the front yard. With a jolt, Hazel dropped the curtain. Memories of corrupt bodies standing frozen around Jen's house reverberated through her mind, beating like her pulse. She grasped the fabric again and pulled it back a crack to peer through.

The figure was still there, its face upturned, waiting for her. Hazel recognized the blonde hair. It was the ghost woman who kept trying to talk to her. Hazel counted her breaths in and out, slowing her heart down. It was just a ghost. The woman was wringing her hands.

Hazel let the curtain shut again. Whatever this woman wanted, Hazel had bigger problems. Why did all ghosts seem to think they were above normal social expectations? It was late. You don't visit someone this late at night. Hazel lifted her used clothes from the floor and dumped them into the laundry basket with an extra huff. Some people had no manners.

15

Chapter 15: Riley

Chapter 15: Riley

The room darkened again as evening fell. Riley tried the walls and door again and again until the room spun. Worries about his mom and Hazel chased each other around in his mind, unresolved. He tried calling up the door he had seen in his house, but either it was a one-time experience, or he was too agitated to do it right.

A door banged downstairs. Riley stiffened, willing it to be rescue and not the man. Ray. The footsteps marched towards his prison. Riley backed towards the far wall, his jaw aching with tension.

Keys turned in the lock. Ray stepped inside wearing the same dark clothes as yesterday, his long hair unwashed. Ray's eyebrows rose and his head tilted to ask if Riley was going to cooperate. Riley folded his arms across his chest.

Ray reached into the inner pocket of his jacket, shaking his head in a slow, dramatic fashion as if Riley was making him do this. Riley glared at the man, pretending he wasn't holding his breath.

Out of the pocket came a tiny, clear object. Ray held it up by a slender chain so Riley could see. It was the jar-charm that Hazel had encouraged Riley to buy and fill with lavender. Riley stared at it, nonplussed.

Without warning, he was ripped forwards. The sensation of a hook in his chest had returned, and somehow Ray's shadow had yanked it. The room disappeared and once again Riley felt the awful compression on all sides. The pressure on his ears was excruciating. He couldn't think straight, he couldn't breathe; everything was wrong.

Then he was on the floor again, gasping for air. He had no idea how long he had been trapped for, but surely he should be dead. Ray towered over him. Riley scrambled to his feet, shaking as if he had a fever. Ray held the necklace aloft.

"This was a lucky find," he said with a smirk. "I want you to remember how it feels to be trapped inside. I could keep you in there forever." He let the word 'forever' hang in that air between them. "Or you could stay in this nice room."

Riley stayed silent, trying to sort his thoughts back into cohesiveness. His heart went on racing, and he couldn't look away from the swaying charm.

Ray smiled. He didn't give Riley enough time to pull himself together. He held the jar to his chest and the shadow's chain jerked Riley forwards again. The room disappeared.

When Riley came to on the floor, Ray was sitting on the edge of the desk, grim satisfaction curling the corner of his mouth.

Riley gulped the air so fast it made his head throb worse than ever. He held up one hand. "Please. Don't."

Ray stood. Riley couldn't do more than sit up as Ray advanced on him, crouching down so they were level. He tucked the jar into his coat pocket. Riley breathed a sigh of relief, but like a flash, the man reached out a finger and touched Riley's temple. Searing fire streaked through every nerve in his body.

When Ray pulled away at last, Riley realized he had been screaming.

"So," Ray said. "Which one was worse?"

Barely able to string a sentence together, Riley managed to say, "What's wrong with you?"

The man raised his shoulders in an innocent shrug and said, "You killed my kin. I should kill you and yours. But I need something from you. So you're going to tell me where the other ghost-seers are, or you'll get to endure more of this."

"Why don't you ask Ray?" Riley dared spit out.

The shadow inside the man smirked. "I've already finished his friends."

Chills ran up and down Riley's arms and spine. He wet his lips, hesitating, but pushed on. "I've met anger shadows and fear shadows before. What kind are you?"

The smirk never left Ray's face. "You humans hate me more than anything. I am the worst kind of pain."

He stood without elaborating and strode to the door. He paused on the threshold and said, "I'll tell your mom you said hi."

It was like a pit opened up inside Riley and his stomach fell through. The door slammed shut, but not before he gave Riley a knowing look. The shadow knew he had him, and it was only a matter of time before Riley cracked.

"No!" Riley cried, stumbling to the door. "Leave her alone! Wait!"

He heard a satisfied sigh on the other side.

***

Riley spent the next hour shivering from his ordeal, pacing, and trying to convince himself that the shadow was only taunting him. He wouldn't really do anything to his mom. But that sigh haunted him.

He called up Sasha's cord, but she wouldn't come. He stared at the other cords instead. Sasha had said not to use them, but they were Riley's only means of communication.

About a month ago, a surly old man with a grey mustache had visited Riley. He had asked a lot of questions about death and life and what was next. When Riley didn't have the answers, he had said, "What good are you then?" and vanished.

Riley couldn't remember his name, but the cord glowed in response to Riley's thoughts.

"Please," Riley sent down the line, "I know you don't know me, and you don't owe me anything, but I need help. Please help me."

He waited, straining his ears for a response. When nothing happened, he whispered a broken, "Please."

"Well, at least you're polite," a voice grumbled.

Riley spun around. The mustached man was standing by the desk, arms folded above his round belly.

Hope burned so strong in Riley's chest that it stung his eyes. "Thank you!" he blurted. "Thank you for coming."

The man frowned, studying the dark office around them. "What is it you need, boy?"

"There's this shadow," Riley said, launching into it as fast as he could, "it eats ghosts and it has me trapped here. It says it's going after my mom. I need to get out of here. And we have to warn all the ghosts to stay away from me."

The man's eyes narrowed as he processed all that information, his arms still folded.

"I can certainly warn away some ghosts," he said at last, "but as for getting you out of here … It appears ghosts can't communicate with the living. Not with ordinary folks."

"I know someone who's not ordinary."

"Really now?"

Riley glanced over his shoulder and lowered his voice just in case. "Her name is Hazel. But she lives in the lower mainland."

"Not a problem," he said. "I suspect I can find her. I sensed you, after all."

"And the distance?"

The man raised a cocky eyebrow. "Ghost, remember?"

Relief made Riley's legs tremble. He thought he might collapse with gratitude. He opened his mouth to thank him, but the man interrupted.

"None of that, boy," he said with a raised hand and a gentle tone. "I can hardly abandon someone in need, can I? I'll be back. Take care of yourself now."

"No!" Riley said.

"What's that?"

"You can't come back. The shadow might get you. Please. Just pass the message along. Stay safe."

The mustached man studied Riley for a long time. Then he said, "Leave it to me."

He vanished.

16

Chapter 16: Kelly

Chapter 16: Kelly

Shadows gathered in the living room, slipping closer and closer to where Logan and Kelly sat on cushions around the coffee table. Kelly felt like banging her head against the surface. They had been arguing for hours, and she could hear her own scream of frustration echoing in her head. She had never argued with someone for so long before. Usually, she would have stormed off by now, and by tomorrow she'd be pretending nothing had happened.

The most she had done tonight was get up and storm around the main floor, but always, she circled back. And Logan was always sitting there, on the couch or on the floor, waiting patiently to continue. Letting her work through her own thoughts. What was it about him that kept bringing her back? It wasn't like he was always calm. His forehead was cupped in his palm now, elbow resting on the coffee table as his frustration gave way to exhaustion.

He looked up at her then, and she didn't look away. They studied each other like anthropologists—so different from each other, but both curious. Somehow, Kelly didn't fear his scrutiny. They were both seeking to understand, not to judge. And it felt like they were getting closer to the centre of the circle.

They both sighed at the same time, which made them crack small smiles.

"So," Logan said, "you can't go on because you feel guilty for not stopping the Shadow when you were a kid."

Kelly nodded. "And you just want to go on because you're lonely and miss your family."

Neither of them flinched from these truths.

"I'm stuck here," Logan said, gesturing to the room at large. Then he put a hand on his heart. "But you're stuck here. Your heart can change. My situation ... can't."

Kelly shook her head. "I think you underestimate the ... *stuckness* of the heart. And I wouldn't want it to change if it meant becoming more selfish. But you. You're not stuck here. You're stuck"—she indicated behind her—"in the past. On relationships that might be ... gone. There's no telling what you'll find through those doors. You can't guarantee your family will be there. Or that you'll even exist there. But you could help me help others."

Logan shook his head and laughed through his nose. "I think I do understand the stuckness of the heart, though, don't I? It's the possibility of seeing my family again that makes me so ..."

They lapsed into silence again. Kelly opened her mouth to speak, but her heartbeat was suddenly racing and it felt like someone had struck a gong in her stomach. The words that were about to come out of her mouth were risky, strong, and somehow permanent.

She said them anyway. "But I'm here. Right now." She couldn't catch her breath, but she forged on. "And ... there are other kinds of family."

Logan's brown eyes locked on hers, and this time she couldn't bear to look at them. Heat was rising in her cheeks as she swung between mortification and pride at her own bravery. Then Logan gasped and leapt to his feet. Kelly spun around to see what he was looking at.

On the other side of the glass patio doors stood a grinning Shadow.

"Guardian," it said. Its voice was gravelly and unfamiliar.

Logan grabbed Kelly's shoulders and pulled her backwards from the door.

"You should not be here," the shadow said.

It walked through the glass towards them. Kelly let out a small yelp and fumbled to find her feet. She and Logan ran straight through the coffee table and raced down the narrow hallway to the front door, stumbling into the walls for balance. The shadow flashed up behind them and Kelly screamed. Logan seized her hand and dragged her out the front door.

The cold night air bit at their faces as they rounded the side of the house, desperate for somewhere to hide. The shadow appeared in front of them, the grin still plastered on its face.

It held out its long fingers, eyes fixed on Logan, and jerked its hand backwards. Logan's feet slid across the grass, pulling him towards it. A rainbow sheen blurred his skin as if the shadow was sucking out his essence. As if he was turning into one of the spirits that soared through the doors.

"No!" Kelly cried, seizing his hand with both of hers.

But the force pulling him forwards was stronger and her feet slid on the frosty grass. The shadow flashed closer, opening its mouth wide to inhale.

"No!" Kelly screamed, and she threw herself in front of Logan, shoving the shadow with both hands.

It was an instinctive reaction, something that might have worked on a solid person, not a shadow. But it didn't matter. It was like she had slammed her hands against invisible glass between them. The air itself shivered. With a crack-like thunder, the sheet of air blasted into the shadow like something solid. The shadow hurtled through the back fence as the force knocked Kelly and Logan to the ground.

Eyes wide with shock, Kelly leapt to her feet and dragged Logan up with her. They didn't waste any time talking. Kelly ran up the invisible steps that allowed them to soar, and together they bolted across the grass and across the street.

Keeping low to the ground for cover, they weaved behind buildings, down alleys, across parking lots, and straight through stores. Kelly began flagging, as if the energy she had blasted at the shadow had taken a toll on her. She forced herself on until they were all the way across town. Then, backs to the wall of an athletics centre, they slipped inside.

"Do you think it can find us?" Logan whispered in the shadow of a leg curl machine.

Kelly shrugged, her jaw so tense a muscle twitched in her cheek. The Shadow she knew had hooks in its targets, but when she tried to feel for them, she found none. Logan held her gaze.

"How did you do that?" he asked.

Kelly opened her mouth, but she had neither words nor any idea how she had done it. She shook her head and looked around instead. They had entered a weight room. The black machines were like hulking beasts. The shadow could be lurking anywhere in this room.

"Let's go somewhere else," she said, and left Logan gaping at her back.

As if he needed more fuel to think she was special somehow. She probably couldn't repeat what she had done to the shadow if she tried.

Logan caught up to her in the wide hallway that led to the reception desk. They passed the reception desk and glass front doors, continuing until they found the pool. It was a long rectangle surrounded by white brick walls. The only natural light came from skylights on the ceiling, but the pool itself was glowing turquoise with underwater lights. Kelly sighed and sat down cross-legged at the water's edge.

Logan settled beside her, letting his shoed feet sink into the water. Kelly bit back her surprise, remembering he could just let the water run off, like he had with the rain.

"So, you have superpowers," he said to his feet.

"I do not."

He looked up at the bite in her voice. "Then what do you call that?"

Kelly stared at her reflection in the water, the familiar blue eyes and chestnut brown hair. The same as in life. "Probably just a ghost thing. I bet you could have done it."

Logan's feet rippled her reflection as he answered, "I don't think so. I've been here a long time now and I've never done something like that."

"Doesn't mean you can't," Kelly insisted, crossing her arms.

Logan gazed at the skylight while the water lapped the pool's edge. "How did you do it?"

Kelly waved her hands in exasperation. "You think I know?"

"Well, what were you thinking? What was going through

your head that made you try it?"

"Nothing!" she exclaimed. Her voice echoed off the walls. "I was just trying to get it away from you and I shoved it like a jackass! I was … scared for you. I panicked."

She glared at the pool so he wouldn't see the colour in her cheeks.

"It called you 'Guardian.' "

She shrugged. "I don't know why. But … this is not the same Shadow I knew."

"It's not?"

Kelly shook her head. "Its voice was different."

Logan frowned. Then he shuddered. "There are more of these things?"

"I guess so." Kelly hugged herself to repress her own shiver.

She thought of Hazel struggling to maintain possession of her Shadow as it ate up her every moment of fear. Could Kelly do that too, if she had no body? She didn't think so, somehow. Besides, Kelly was not brave like Hazel. The corner of her lips lifted in a rueful smile. The Shadow would probably be too well fed under her watch.

Still, Kelly felt a sort of buoyancy in her chest, a solidifying of hope. If she could repeat that moment in the yard, maybe she could prevent the shadow from taking more souls. Maybe she could starve it by preventing it from feeding. Maybe this was the answer. Maybe, at last, she had a way to fight back. She just needed to figure out how to do it again. She swallowed her stubbornness and climbed, groaning, to her feet.

"How long do you think we'll have to hide out here?" Logan asked as she rose. "Do you think it will find us?"

"If I *can* do that again," she said, "it won't matter."

Logan sat up straighter. Kelly looked around the pool for

something she could practice on, but all the pool noodles and floaties were hidden away in a cupboard somewhere. She turned to Logan.

"Can I try it on you?"

He put a hand to his heart like he was clutching pearls. "Me?"

She almost laughed. "There's nothing else to use. You can practice on me too."

Logan got up, the water sloughing off his shoes until they were dry.

"Will it hurt?"

Kelly grimaced. "I don't know."

Logan moved so that his back was to the pool. "In that case, I'll stand here so the landing is soft."

Kelly smiled. "I don't deserve you," she said before she could stop herself.

Logan caught his breath, then started babbling, "My mom used to say that too. But only when I was being nice. Whenever I didn't want to clean my room or if I was dragging my feet about going somewhere, she'd say, 'The devil take this child,' and roll her eyes. If I really annoyed her, she'd throw her hands up like this"—he waved both hands at the ceiling, grinning in fond memory—"and walk away. But I knew it was really bad if she middle-named me. Did you ever get middle-named? Once I was jumping on the couch and—"

"Logan." Kelly arched an eyebrow.

"Oh, right," he said sheepishly, then raised his hands and scrunched up his face as if bracing himself to get hit.

Kelly laughed. "You're not helping."

"Okay, okay, I'll be serious," he agreed, still grinning.

Kelly had to look down at her feet and take a deep breath to shake her laughter. She stared at the pool tiles and put herself back in the moment where the shadow had started to drag Logan away. She saw the colours fleeing from his skin. Her stomach dipped at the memory. She raised her hands in self-defence, pretending the shadow stood before her, not Logan, and imagined it opening its jaws.

"No!" she cried, and shoved Logan's chest.

He stumbled backwards, teetering on the edge of the pool. Kelly's voice was still echoing off the walls when he regained his balance. Her shoulders slumped. Even that move had sapped her energy.

"Sorry."

Logan waved her apology away. "Try again."

They returned to their starting positions. Kelly's cheeks reddened as she prepared to try again. She raised her hands again, cried, "No!" and imagined her hands striking the air. Instead, she hit Logan. He recovered better this time, only taking one step towards the pool.

"Maybe it was a one-time thing," she said, shame curling in her stomach as her echoes died away.

"Nah." Logan was confident. "I think you're getting in your own head. Stop worrying about how it sounds, and definitely don't worry about me. I'm the enemy right now. I'm the shadow. You're trying to protect us from it. Or someone you care about. Try again."

Kelly nodded, her brow furrowing with concentration. She imagined Logan, Hazel, and her best friend, Di, all standing behind her. She imagined Gran and her mom; all the people she had lost. She felt a little spark of anger. She would have done anything to protect these people, if it weren't too late.

"No!" she shouted and launched herself at Logan.

She shoved him hard enough to push him into the pool even

without any ghost powers. But just before her hands touched his chest, they struck solid air. A thunderclap sounded in the tiny room, and the air slammed against Logan. He was blasted backwards 10 feet before he crashed into the water.

Kelly gasped and ran to the pool's edge. Her ears were ringing as she knelt, waiting for Logan to resurface. He came up choking.

"Whoooo!" he cheered, sinking back under as he raised his fists in celebration.

Kelly beamed. Logan had not flown as far as the shadow had, but it worked! They had a way to fight back and even the playing field. She could protect the souls who came through this layer hoping to move on. Tears sprang to her eyes. At last, she could help.

Logan swam back over to her, and she offered her hand to pull him out. He crawled over the ledge and got to his feet, dripping water, but then he shook like a dog and it reversed back into the pool, leaving him as dry as Kelly. She laughed, but when she met his eyes, they were dancing with pride. She clasped her hands together to stop herself from throwing her arms around him.

"Your turn," she said.

"I can't do that!" Logan laughed.

"We won't know that until you've tried," she challenged. "Trade places with me."

She stood at the pool's edge as he wavered.

"Come on!" she insisted.

Logan sighed, but his grin betrayed him. "I do owe you for throwing me into the pool."

17

Chapter 17: Hazel

Hazel tossed and turned, watching the clock eat away at her night. At 4:00am she gave up and crept downstairs to watch TV and hopefully fall asleep on the couch. After gathering blankets around her, she peered between the blinds behind the couch. To her surprise, not only was the ghost woman still out there, but she was gesturing at the house as she conversed with a round, mustached man.

Hazel let the blinds snap shut before they could catch sight of her. She was tempted to go outside and tell them off. This woman could *not* take a hint. And now there was a man too. Hazel jabbed the power button for the TV a little harder than necessary, then stabbed at the volume down button. She kept her eyes on the TV for the rest of the night.

***

Hazel spent the next day yawning nonstop. She had two classes, but the gap between them was big enough to squeeze in a short run and shower. As she jogged around the block for her warm-up, the female and male ghosts waved at her. Hazel put in her earbuds, pulled up her hood, and ignored them. They followed her from a distance the entire time, looking angrier each time she diverted her eyes. It got so uncomfortable that Hazel opened the jar of lavender to repel them further.

Usually, Hazel felt happy and accomplished after a run. Today she snapped the door shut behind her. Resolved in bringing up these ghosts at her evening meeting, Hazel showered and tried to put them out of her mind.

When her class got out at 3:50, Hazel saw the message from Riley. She had just made it into the hallway, her bag slung over one shoulder, when she registered his name on her phone. Her heart leapt into her throat. She dropped all her belongings by the wall, tapping her phone until her messages popped up. There was one from Riva checking in on her, but she bypassed it and pulled up the one from Riley with bated breath.

"Hey," it read. "Can I get your address?"

Hazel stared. She read it again, sure she had missed something. Then she typed with the speed of an angry hailstorm.

"Does this mean you're okay? Are you still at the hospital? What's going on? What happened to you?" She hit send, then added, "Why do you need my address?"

She waited with her eyes fixed on the screen like the phone would disappear if she blinked. Finally, he responded.

"I'm fine. I'm still at the hospital. But I need to send you something."

"Did your mom tell you about the shadow? What do the doctors think is happening?" She texted her address, then asked, "What are you sending me?"

There was a long pause this time. Hazel nodded to the last of her classmates as they filtered past. Then he replied to the question about his mom: "She did, but I'd like to hear it from you."

So Hazel spilled the whole story over text, right down to the visitors congregating around her house and bed. She walked to her car while she waited for his response. He took so long that she was already settling into the driver's seat when her phone buzzed.

His response read, "I think you should talk to the ghosts. Get rid of the lavender."

Hazel frowned. She stared out at the parking lot over her steering wheel. It seemed unlikely that the ghosts would know something about all this. They were just lost souls looking for guidance. She twisted the rubber of the steering wheel under her hands, remembering how she had treated them.

Finally, she replied, "I'll ask the girls what they think tonight. We're having a team meeting." When Riley didn't reply, she added, "I'm just driving home. I'm so glad you're okay. You have no idea."

***

Hazel spent the rest of the afternoon picking up and dropping her textbook. She invited Riley to video call in to the meeting at 7:00pm, but he hadn't sent anything since his text about the ghosts. She hoped his condition hadn't worsened, but she refrained from peppering him with personal questions he didn't seem to want to answer. She napped instead, sleep coming to her at last.

When 7:00pm arrived, Hazel, Jen, and Kate were all waiting on the couch, while Riva sat in the armchair fiddling with her dark braids. At the sound of the doorbell, Kate bounced to her feet to answer.

"Hey!" she greeted their guests, throwing her arms around Di's neck, then Morgan's.

Di's hug was all warmth, while Morgan patted Kate on the

back. Morgan's warmth came in the form of a six pack of coolers which she held aloft. "My mom said never arrive empty-handed."

Kate grinned and handed out the drinks. Morgan led Di to the armchair Riva offered. Morgan and Riva settled on cushions on the floor. When the greetings and catching up seemed unlikely to ever end, Jen cleared her throat, and all eyes immediately swivelled to Hazel.

"Like I said in our group chat," Hazel said, "Riley messaged me today. He's out of his coma."

The girls cheered and Kate raised her drink. They clinked their cans together over the coffee table.

"So does this mean the shadow gave up on him?" Riva asked.

Hazel shook her head. "I doubt it." She took a deep breath and rushed on, "I think we need to be proactive this time. I think *we* should go after *it.* Kate, Riley, and I."

"Yeah!" Kate cheered again. This time no one joined her. She stared around at them all. "Well, come on. People got hurt the longer we waited last time. This is our chance to take a shadow down before it knows we're coming."

"But it put Riley in a coma," Jen said, shifting in her seat to speak directly to Hazel. "The others weren't able to do that."

"I know," Hazel agreed. "But—"

"And," Morgan added, tucking her short dark hair behind her ear, "Riley is probably weaker from the attack. He might not be able to pull it off this time."

"It'll take us some time to drive out to him," Hazel pointed out. "But, yes, there's some risk that he won't be recovered. But we're talking about people's lives, or souls, or whatever. We have to try. I think Riley will agree."

Riva, who had been quiet so far, opened her mouth to speak,

but Jen beat her to it. "I think you're forgetting the stakes here. If it goes wrong, we're talking about *your* souls."

Di piped up from the armchair, her unseeing eyes turned in Hazel's direction. "I think you need to talk to Riley some more. Maybe he can give us some insight into how this thing got him and what it wants. Has he said anything?"

"Not since this afternoon when he told me he was up. But he did give me some advice about something else. I want to know your thoughts about that too."

Hazel told them about the ghosts stalking her and how Riley thought she should ditch the lavender and find out what they wanted.

"I don't know," Jen said. "Like you said, they are being rude."

"They're not entitled to your time," Morgan agreed.

"But I'm one of the few people they can talk to," Hazel pointed out. "Doesn't that mean I have a responsibility to—"

There was a resounding "No!" from around the room.

Hazel pretended to flinch back, grinning. Then she forged on, "But I understand where they're coming from. Imagine you died, and you could see your loved ones but you couldn't talk to them. Then you find me."

Jen sighed and put a gentle hand on Hazel's knee. "Hazel, we've talked about this. You are not responsible for everyone else. You have to let go of that guilt. There are too many people on this planet for you to help. It's literally impossible. Feeling guilty for being human, for being one person, is ridiculous."

Hazel ran a hand through her hair. "It's just ... I've never blocked ghosts off to this extent before. Maybe they'll just keep piling up outside the house until there's a whole crowd of them rioting and stalking me."

Jen blanched at the suggestion.

"If this isn't working for you," Riva declared as if she might not be heard, "then you can change it. It's not up to us. We're only asking you to keep ghosts out of the house. If you want to talk to them out in the world, that's fine. But we also want you to consider your own mental health. School is a lot to have on your plate without this unpaid obligation."

"Yeah," Morgan agreed. "You need boundaries."

"But it's up to you where you put them," Riva went on, throwing a dark braid over her shoulder. "If these ghosts are bothering you and you don't want to wait them out, then you should go talk to them. You can always tell them to leave."

Hazel imagined getting a restraining order against a ghost, then laughed to herself. In a way, that's what the lavender was.

"If they're being rude, you don't owe them anything," Jen argued, "not even a conversation."

Hazel toyed with the tab on her drink until it broke off.

"Think about it," Di said into the silence. "We're here for you, whatever you decide."

Around the room, all the girls agreed. Jen put her arm over Hazel's shoulder and gave her a squeeze. Hazel smiled.

"So," Kate said from her corner of the couch, "back to the Riley thing. Can you call him? I think he should be part of this, now that he's awake."

Hazel pulled out her phone and dialed Riley as the girls had whispered side conversations. When she got his voicemail, she hung up.

"Nothing?" Kate asked.

"Nothing," Hazel confirmed. "Maybe I'll try his mom, just to make sure he's okay."

Elisabeth's return text was immediate. "He's the same. I'll let you know if anything changes. Have you had any more ideas?"

Hazel informed her about the brainstorming session and promised she'd update her if they came up with anything. Her phone vibrated.

"Riley says he can't talk right now," Hazel read to the group.

"Well," Di said, "my thought is, don't do anything until we have more information from Riley. I'm sorry, Hazel, I know that's not what you want to hear."

Hazel laughed through her nose. "Don't be sorry. But. I do think we should talk logistics about Kate and me getting out to Riley tomorrow or the next day if he gets back to me soon. Just in case we want to go with the element-of-surprise plan."

The girls spent the rest of the night discussing the logistics of driving out to Riley in case they wanted to go with the surprise-the-shadow plan. Mixed in was catching up and laughter. Hazel watched her friends sipping drinks and smiling, and it once again struck her how lucky they were to be alive and in the same room. Gratitude warmed her as she leaned into the couch.

Then the sadness that always followed hit. She imagined Kelly was a part of this group, sitting with Di, her former best friend. Kelly, laughing along with the others. She wondered if they would have combined their friend groups like this. Or if Kelly would be living here instead of Kate. Maybe the house would be full of the half-empty glasses Kelly was notorious for leaving in every room. Would the two sisters have grown closer as they grew up? Hazel wished they had had a chance to find out. As it was, she thought Kelly would smile if she could see how things turned out. The sadness wasn't as strong as it used to be.

***

Hazel woke to the buzz of a text at 1:00am. She fumbled for

her phone on the nightstand and tilted it towards her until she could read Riley's name. Tucking it under the blanket so the light wouldn't wake Jen, she read, "Sorry I couldn't answer earlier, I was driving. I was coming to see you, but I'm lost and now my car is steaming. Can you pick me up?"

Hazel texted back, "You're here??"

"I'm sorry it's so late," he replied. "I tried to make it to your meeting, but the drive took longer than I expected."

Hazel closed her eyes against the bright light, trying to assemble her sleepy thoughts. Then she messaged back, "Where are you? Do you see any street signs?"

"Hillcrest Drive," Riley texted back.

Hazel pulled up a map. She rubbed her eyes when she saw Hillcrest, wondering if she could convince him to call a cab. Then she sighed and wrote, "You're definitely lost. It'll probably take me about 20 minutes to get there."

Hazel climbed out from under the covers, using the light from her phone to locate some clothes. She was dressed and reached for the lavender necklace on her nightstand, but hesitated. Maybe Riva was right, and she should just tell the ghosts to leave her alone. She grabbed it in her fist but didn't put it on.

On the stairs she got one more message from Riley saying, "Thank you! I'm really sorry about this."

All the lights were out in the house, and the girls were fast asleep, so Hazel crept into the kitchen to leave a note. She left it on the table, explaining where she was going in case anyone missed her. Then she slipped out to her car.

18

Chapter 18: Riley

The pain and compression transcended consciousness. Riley could only feel the suffocation; he had no thoughts, no self, only misery. When it ended, he lay on a plywood surface, gasping for air. His self didn't immediately come back, even as he registered the metal walls, and sensed his hands and feet. It was only when he feared he had lost his sanity that relief returned. Fearing for his sanity was a thought, and it brought him back.

He turned his head without rising, and there above him hovered a shadow. Ray.

Ray *hmphed* with satisfaction. "Good. I didn't know if you'd survive it this far from your body."

Riley let his cheek drop back to the plywood floor.

"I've bound you to this truck now," Ray said, knocking on the floor, "so we won't need the jar anymore. But there's still some way to go. You might not make it. You might get torn apart. Sound familiar?"

With a sneer, he stood, his boots clunking on the wood as he strode away. Riley felt the floor lift when he jumped out of

109

the truck, then he heard the sliding door slam down. *A moving truck*, his slow thoughts told him.

The truck rumbled to life, vibrating Riley's teeth. The roof was lost in darkness. Riley felt like he was floating in a state of death. Like a lingering nightmare, he couldn't shake the experience of the jar. He wished he could see something, anything, to convince him he was real—alive—and sane. The truck gave a lurch, swaying before it accelerated onto a smoother road.

That's when a blue light appeared somewhere near Riley's feet. He forced himself into a sitting position. The sliding door of the truck was open a crack. He crawled towards it, grasping the looped strap that dangled from the door and acted as a handle. His hand didn't go through it; it was as solid as the floor. With all his might, Riley wrenched the door upwards.

Blue light washed over his body, and he stared in shock. He was not looking at a road. He was looking at a pool. Even as the truck swayed, the pool water remained still and calm. Then he saw the body. A teen girl about his age was lying at the water's edge, her eyes staring up at the ceiling.

"Hello?" Riley whispered.

The girl's eyes snapped over to him and she sat bolt upright, making Riley gasp and clutch his already taxed heart.

"It's you!" she said. "I saw you before!"

Her voice sounded blurred again, like something was separating them. Riley inched closer to the door on his knees, fearing that if he crossed the boundary, he would fall out of the truck and die on the road.

"Who are you?" he asked.

"Kelly," she said, hurrying over to kneel across from him. "Who are you?"

"Riley," he told her. Her name stirred something in his memory, but he hardly dared to believe it. "You were calling for Hazel before. The last time I saw you."

The girl nodded. "My sister. I've been looking for her."

Her eyes. They were the precise shade of Hazel's. "You … you died in a zombie attack."

Her eyes popped and she inched even closer, nodding. "Yes! I did. How did you know that?"

"I know your sister," Riley said. "I know Hazel."

Kelly's whole face lit up with excitement. She slapped her hands on her thighs. "Get out!"

Riley smiled for the first time in days. Kelly took in his surroundings like she thought Hazel would be there with him.

"Where are you?" she asked.

Riley's smile slipped away. "I'm in trouble," he admitted. "You know about shadows, right?"

Kelly's smile vanished too. "There's one here."

It was Riley's turn to be surprised. "Oh. I'm sorry."

Kelly nodded her thanks. "Logan's on watch for it. He's a … a friend I made over here."

"Where exactly—" Riley began, but he interrupted himself. He didn't have time for questions. He didn't know how long he had, and he needed help. "Can you get in touch with Hazel for me?"

Kelly sagged and her face fell. "I was hoping you could."

A voice interrupted them. It was Ray speaking from the cab of the truck. Riley raised a hand to stop Kelly for a moment and leaned toward the sound, straining his ears to hear. He made out the phrase, "Text Hazel," but couldn't make out much of the rest. It sounded like Ray was using voice-to-text.

After a long pause, Ray spoke again. "Text Hazel: Hillcrest

Drive."

A thrill of terror clenched his insides. "I think he has my phone. He must have visited my mom after all!"

Riley couldn't repress a shudder as the image of Elisabeth lying unconscious on the hospital floor flashed across his mind. He ran his hands over his face, panic rising. But there was nothing he could do for his mom. He was stuck in this truck, with only Kelly to help him. With a wrench, he pulled his thoughts back to Hazel. She was in danger now, and he could do something about that.

"It sounds like he's meeting Hazel at Hillcrest Drive," Riley said, twisting back to face Kelly. "We have to stop her. What if you come through and go visit her as a ghost?"

Kelly put her hand to the air between them, her palm flattening. The air rippled at her touch, just like before. "I can't, remember?"

Riley raised his hand to touch the surface, too, his fingers inches away before a voice behind him cried, "No, don't!"

He whipped around. Kelly shrieked.

Sasha was standing in the corner. She dashed across the plywood floor and dropped to her knees beside Riley. Kelly leapt to her feet in alarm.

"You can only cross over if you're dead!" she said. "What if touching it kills you?"

Riley jerked his hand back.

"Who is that?" Kelly demanded, her voice a higher pitch.

"It's okay," Riley said. "This is Sasha. She's a ghost."

Kelly looked like she was debating whether that made it okay. She hovered where she stood, her eyes wary.

"I thought you couldn't be here while he was awake," Riley said to Sasha.

Sasha nodded, her face tense. "They'll know. But he can't come after me while he's driving. And *you* almost killed yourself! It seemed worth it."

The truck made an abrupt turn and slowed. Riley threw his hands out for balance, his heart accelerating.

"How do you know he'll die if he crosses over?" Kelly asked. She was frowning like she didn't trust Sasha at all.

"Through Ray's friends," Sasha said. "He has—had—this online friend group. People all over the world who could communicate with the dead. They shared all sorts of knowledge. One of them," she said to Riley, "said his ancestor was a Traveller, like you. He said she died crossing over. Her soul never came back."

"What does that mean, Traveller?" Riley spoke fast as the truck came to a jerking stop. "He called me that before."

"It means you can dream-walk. You can leave your body and see into the next world." Sasha indicated the pool on the other side of the door. Her mouth drooped with regret. "You might even be the last one."

Then she met Kelly's eyes and tipped her head. "But you ... you, I've never heard of. The Travellers always said the other side looked empty."

The truck door slammed. Sasha and Riley jumped as if struck and exchanged fearful expressions.

"The shadow called me a Guardian," Kelly said, unaware of the danger Riley and Sasha were in.

Sasha snapped back to Kelly, "You've seen it?"

"I sort of ... attacked it. With energy."

Sasha's eyes darted side to side as she thought fast. "But you can't be a Guardian then. It doesn't make sense."

Footsteps on gravel. They were out of time. Sasha turned

her face back to the other world, the blue light bathing her in a ghostly glow. Pain flickered across her face.

To Riley she said, "You can't go, but I can. Maybe Ray will reject the shadow then."

She rose to her feet, but at that moment the door of the truck was thrown upwards, and the door to the other side came crashing down.

"No!" Riley cried as the blue light vanished and Kelly was cut off from view.

Sasha screamed and clutched at her chest. She was wrenched forwards by the shadow's chain until Ray held her by the front of her shirt, her feet dangling over the broken pavement. Ray's lips curled into a ravenous sneer.

"No, don't!" Riley cried, leaping to his feet. He forgot about the truck's invisible chains, and they caught him around the middle as he rushed the open door. He fell back, the wind knocked out of him.

Something flickered in Ray's face. Through clenched teeth he muttered to himself, "We had a deal! You wouldn't harm her if I let you in."

"Ray, please!" Sasha begged.

Ray's chin lowered, and he glared at Sasha from under his eyebrows, looking positively murderous.

"She tried to leave you, Ray."

"No!" Sasha cried. "I'm trying to help you!"

"She tried to save herself," the shadow spat at Sasha.

"No!" she cried again. "Please, Ray, I love you! Please. Please don't let it take me."

Riley strained against the chains he couldn't see, trying to find a weak spot in the open door, but he was helpless to save Sasha.

Tears rolled down Sasha's face. "Please," she whispered.

Ray's hand opened the tiniest fraction. Sasha dropped to her feet, vanishing in an instant. Safe. Then the shadow turned a murderous gaze on Riley. Riley wasted no time backing deeper into the truck, but Ray leapt inside with one hand. Riley's back hit the far wall as Ray advanced on him. He reached out a hand and touched Riley's temple. Riley screamed.

19

Chapter 19: Kelly

The door came crashing down and somehow up at the same time. Then Kelly was staring at the white brick walls. She couldn't help herself; she patted the cold bricks as if searching for a secret door. When nothing gave, she sat back, her mind spinning.

Hazel was dealing with another shadow, and there was nothing Kelly could do to help her. Her hope had shot so high when she learned Riley knew her sister, and crashed so much further. The low felt like a gut-punch.

"Hillcrest Drive," Kelly said aloud, her voice echoing.

She knew that winding street. Di lived near that street, in the middle of the hill. Kelly pictured a shadow prowling outside Di's house, using her to lure Hazel, and her heart clenched with fear. She had to do something. Even if she was in another layer of reality, she would go to Hillcrest in solidarity and try to send her support through the air, the layer, from heart-to-heart—whatever it took.

She sprinted across the pool deck and changeroom, then down the deserted halls of the gym in search of Logan. She found him peering through the glass windows of the squash courts as if expecting to find the shadow playing a match on the other side.

"Logan!" she called.

He jumped and swore.

"I just saw a door and talked to one of Hazel's friends," Kelly said as fast as she could. "He says there's another shadow and it's trying to lure Hazel to Hillcrest Drive. I have to go!"

"What? Who? You can't go out! There's a shadow out there somewhere hoping to lure *us* out!"

Kelly didn't entertain his concerns. "I'm going."

She turned to leave, but he caught her wrist. "But what can you do? You're just putting yourself in danger. Would Hazel really want—"

"It's not about what she would want," Kelly interrupted. "It's about what she would do for me."

She looked him dead in the eye, refusing to blink until he released his hold on her wrist.

"You have to do this," he realized.

"Yes."

"Okay." He nodded once. "Let's go."

She raised her eyebrows in surprise. "You should stay hidden."

A corner of Logan's mouth turned up in a sly grin. "I'm safest with the superhero."

Heat flushed Kelly's cheeks faster than she could control. She turned on her heel so he wouldn't see.

"Fine. Let's go."

She could sense that he was smiling more than ever, but she stuffed the flattered butterflies in her stomach down.

Taking the shortest route, Kelly cut straight through all the walls until they were out in the dark street. Without streetlights, the town was so black the shadow could be beside them and they wouldn't know. Kelly hesitated. Her original thought, to cut straight across town, suddenly seemed reckless. She strode into the middle of the street.

"What are you doing?" Logan hissed from the sidewalk.

"It's a toss-up," Kelly replied. "The shadow might see us better, but if it comes out, the moonlight will at least tip us off."

Logan made a worried growl, but followed her. They ran up the invisible steps into the air, Kelly leading towards the northeast side of town. Here, businesses started to get scarce and the household yards grew bigger. She tried to reach for Hazel in her mind, calling her name with all her heart, telling her not to go to Hillcrest. Without a cord to communicate down and no door to speak through, all Kelly could do was will the message to reach her.

The town flew by under Kelly's feet until she set down at a run on Di's street. They were on a little mountain, populated by both old and modern houses. The road ran parallel to the view. If Kelly looked between the houses and evergreen trees, she could see the green farmland down below that the valley was famous for.

Di's house was a common '70s construction called a BC box, named after the province it was built in. Kelly didn't need to go inside to know that on the other side of its flat front was a set of stairs going up to the living room, and another going down to the basement. What she needed to know was if there was a shadow inside.

She stared at the houses, trying to catch her breath. Logan, meanwhile, was looking down the length of the road to where it curved around a corner.

"Um ... Kelly?"

"What is it?" she asked, already dreading the answer.

"Did you know there's a cemetery over there?"

Kelly's eyes locked on the glimpse of gravestones she could see at the end of the road. She had forgotten.

"Do you think that's why the shadow chose this place?"

Kelly swallowed and said the morbid thought that popped into her head: "Lots of ghosts to snack on ..."

They exchanged a nervous grimace, squared their shoulders, and set out for the graveyard.

20

Chapter 20: Hazel

Hazel lowered the gear as her car worked its way up Hillcrest Drive. On her right was a hilly graveyard. Her car hugged the corner as she followed the cemetery's curve up the hill. Houses began to appear on the left. Before the road could curve farther to the left and leave the cemetery behind, Hazel slowed the car and pulled over. The only other vehicle around was a white moving truck just ahead.

She took out her phone to call Riley and find out exactly where he was, but the phone rang and rang. Rather than look at the graves to her right, Hazel's eyes settled on the jar of lavender in the cupholder. She clutched the necklace in her fist, the chain spilling out between her fingers. There was a reason she had three urns sitting on her bedroom windowsill.

When Riley still didn't answer, Hazel turned her reluctant gaze to the graveyard. She had parked in front of a black gate with a low brick wall on either side that cut off as if someone had abandoned the job. Most of the gravestones on the rolling hill were flat plaques on the ground, but a few jutted into the night air. To her surprise, the whole hill appeared deserted, not a ghost in sight.

She sent Riley a text, but when she looked up from her phone, she spotted a figure silhouetted at the top of the hill near a leafless tree. She squinted to see it better. The figure raised its hand in a wave. Hazel sat back in her seat, frowning. She couldn't tell if it was Riley or a ghost waving at her. There had been a suspicious lack of ghosts tonight. Even outside her house the woman had been absent, and there was no sign of the new man.

"I'm not coming up there, Riley," Hazel muttered to herself. "If that's you, you better come down here."

But the figure waved more insistently, and when Hazel didn't move, it raised both palms to the sky in a 'What are you waiting for?' gesture. It was Riley, alright. Hazel sighed and let her head hit the backrest before unbuckling her seatbelt. Riley was about to get an earful for making her walk into a graveyard in the middle of the night.

Lavender gripped tight in her fist, Hazel left the safety of her car. She passed the boundary wall next to the gate, her head on a swivel until she reached the plaques and had to keep her head down so she wouldn't trip. Up the hill she climbed, her breath creating a fog in front of her face. When next she looked up, Riley had disappeared from the hilltop.

"Riley?" she called.

Her voice cut across the open grass, and she glanced around, checking for a security guard who might chase them away. The whole field was deserted. Riley didn't respond, and Hazel stopped walking, listening to her gut. Even if Riley laughed at her in a minute, Hazel remembered her mom telling her it was always better to be safe than sorry.

"Riley, come back!" she ordered, planting her feet and

crossing her arms for warmth.

There was a moment of silence. Then two new silhouettes appeared on the crest of the hill, both on their knees facing her. Hazel couldn't make out their faces. She took a step back.

The first figure climbed back over the hill and stopped between the two kneeling ghosts. "Hazel," it said. "Run, and I will consume them."

The blood drained from Hazel's face as her heart pulsed dread to the tips of her fingers. She had never heard this voice before.

She swallowed and croaked, "Where's Riley?"

The man before her laughed and tilted his head to the side. His message was clear: You should be worried about yourself.

"What do you want?" she spat.

He took a step closer, and Hazel answered with a step back. The man pulled both hands forwards as if yanking at something invisible, and the ghosts were jerked face down onto the dirt. Hazel froze, remembering his threat. She could see their distressed faces now and recognized the two ghosts from her front yard. Had this man been to her house? Her skin prickled as every hair stood on end. The woman tried to call out to Hazel, but the lavender clenched in Hazel's hand was working its magic.

Hazel gave the man the dirtiest look she could muster. "Who are you?"

"This human is called Ray," he said, gesturing down his torso. His smile showed his bottom teeth, like he was ready to chew her up and spit her out. "He helps me find you."

"And why did you want to find me?" Hazel asked, refusing to show her unease.

He tipped his head the other way and studied her as if wondering how much to say. "My meals keep getting away," he said at last. "I have to close the doors."

Hazel frowned at this incomprehensible explanation. He took another step towards her, and Hazel's anger flared. She held the lavender jar up for him to see, yanked off the lid, and took a threatening step towards him. The ghosts at his side vanished. Hazel smirked.

His eyes took in the missing ghosts and snapped back to Hazel. He ground his teeth. "I still have my hooks in them. They won't get far."

He lunged. His position at the top of the hill gave him the upper hand, and Hazel didn't have time to run. With a gasp, she dodged to the right, pivoting on one foot. She saw the flash of a knife at the last second and curved her body to avoid its edge. Ray took several more stumbling steps before he could stop himself.

He was between her and the car. Hazel didn't waste a second. She bolted to the top of the hill and raced along its peak towards the houses on Hillcrest Drive. Ray chased after her from below, his long legs making it easy to leap over the plaques on the ground. Hazel pushed harder, trusting her strong thighs to keep her out of his range. Her mind was spinning over what had just happened: *He tried to stab me.*

"Help!" she hollered at the houses. "Someone—"

The knife flew through the air in front of her nose and Hazel cut off with a gasp, skidding on the wet grass. This man was a *psychopath.* He raced up the hill, pressing his advantage. Hazel was forced to run down the opposite side, towards the newer graves. Knowing her best bet was to get help, she screamed at the top of her lungs. No words, just sheer, mind-splitting volume that spread out across the cemetery like a drop of blood in water, tiny, but impossible to miss.

Ray threw himself at Hazel, seizing her around the knees. She crashed to the ground. The blow stole her breath, leaving only the echo of her scream in the air. The lavender necklace flew from her hand.

Ray crawled towards her throat. Hazel hooked his leg with one of hers and knocked both his reaching hands to one side. She planted her other leg and thrust upwards with that hip as she lunged into a hug that tipped him sideways. She didn't wait to pin him as he rolled onto his back. She had to get out of here.

As she ran, Ray dove for her ankle. He managed to grasp the leg of her pants, but it was enough. Hazel tripped and fell, her head striking the edge of a plaque. Bright specks danced across her vision. She scrambled up, but the blow disoriented her, and she stumbled to her knees. Ray's arm wrapped around her neck in a headlock, cutting off her air.

More bright lights blurred her vision. They gathered at the edges, leaving a perfect tunnel in the middle. Through the tunnel was a door standing open among the gravestones. Hazel struggled against Ray's grip, but he squeezed harder. Weakness overtook her, and the door stood out more clearly. Hazel could make out two figures inside.

"You asked where Riley was," Ray breathed in her ear. "Maybe you'll see him on the other side."

A thrill of horror ran through Hazel. Had this man killed Riley? Had she been too late to help him? Blood pounded in her head as her last hopeless thought slipped away.

"Hazel!" a distant voice cried.

As the tunnel of stars closed in around the door, Hazel saw who had called her name. Kelly was running towards her even as the wood along the doorframe fractured. Kelly threw her hands over her head to shield herself from the flying splinters as she crossed over. Then whoever was behind Kelly caught her by the elbow and pulled her back. The door was about to slam shut. Kelly's hair flew around her face as she turned back to Hazel, one hand reaching for her.

"I love you!" she shouted, straining to reach her sister.

Hazel's vision went dark, but she felt a surge of love at hearing her sister's voice, at hearing the words she would have given anything to hear just yesterday.

Suddenly, her cheek was on the wet grass. The man had released her. Hazel gasped for air, clutching her throat and coughing. She fought her light-headedness and sat up. Ray was lying on the ground, seizing like he'd been electrocuted. Hazel leapt to her feet and bolted, leaving him there on top of someone's grave.

Lights were on in a house across the street. Hazel could see someone peering through the front window, searching for the source of the scream. With energy she shouldn't have had, Hazel sprinted over the plaques and leapt over headstones, waving with all her might. The neighbour hurried out to the road to meet her, a phone pressed to their ear.

21

Chapter 21: Riley

Banging on the sides of the parked truck had done absolutely nothing to attract attention. Riley had heard the sound of a car door shut, followed by someone's footsteps, but they heard nothing from him. Then a scream sent a ripple of cold down Riley's spine, and he knew without a doubt it was Hazel. Ray and the shadow had succeeded in luring her out. Riley's brain faltered over what that scream could only mean.

He scratched at the walls, screamed for help, and tore at his hair when nothing helped. Then he heard the truck's driver-side door open. The engine started and the tires squealed as the truck spun a tight U-turn and tore away. Riley crashed against the wall, and he had to lie flat on the ground to stop himself from being thrown around.

The wild driving went on for twenty minutes. At last, Riley heard gravel under the tires, and the truck came to a stop. He rose to his feet, wiping his sweating palms on his thighs. Ray climbed out of the cab and paced over the gravel. When his footsteps made their way to the backdoor, Riley backed away.

Ray shoved the door open.

To Riley's surprise, Ray climbed inside and pulled the door down behind him. Riley hardly dared to breathe in the dark, trapped with a shadow. Ray sat next to the door with a groan, leaning his back against the wall. He ran his hands over his face. The gesture was so human, Riley could only stare.

It was a long time before Ray's eyes settled on Riley.

"You don't have to fear me," he said, his voice low. "The shadow is ... on the other side."

Riley frowned but didn't speak. Did he mean the shadow was dead?

As if his silence was an accusation, Ray said, "I did this for her!"

Riley swallowed and ventured, "But did she want this?"

"The other option was to be obliterated!" Ray hissed. "I can't let that happen to her. I can't let it have her. I can't lose her!" His voice cracked with emotion.

"Sasha told me ... she doesn't want *this* for *you*," Riley pressed.

Ray buried his face in his hands again. His shoulders shook.

Riley steeled himself and crossed the truck. He knelt in front of Ray. "This way, you're both hurting. You need to let her go. If the shadow is gone, this is her chance. Do it now."

Ray lifted his eyes to meet Riley's. All Riley saw was a man in pain. Sympathy curled in his stomach. It was easier to call up a door this time. The blue glow of the pool illuminated the truck's interior. He could see the sheen of sweat on Ray's brow.

"If you love her, let her go," Riley said.

Ray nodded once, tears filling his eyes. Then he gasped, his hands convulsing into fists.

"What's happening?" Riley demanded. His hands lifted,

looking for some way to help.

"It's coming back through the door," Ray said, his face scrunching up as if resisting.

Riley's eyes flew to the pool, but there was no one there. When he looked back at Ray, his face had morphed from pain to fury as fast as flicking a light switch. Riley stumbled backwards, and the door he was holding open in his mind vanished. Ray stood. He stalked towards Riley, looming over him.

"Your friend is dead," he spat. "Did you hear her screams? And it was all thanks to you." He held Riley's phone aloft.

Riley's eyes latched onto the phone, but all he could think about was Hazel's scream and the way it had chilled him.

"No," he said. "She can't be dead."

Ray only smiled as if Riley was being cute. Riley did not like the implication. Desperate, he tried to call up Hazel's cord, but the next thing he knew, a jolt of electricity shot up his neck as Ray seized Riley's face in his hands. But unlike before, the pain flickered and was gone. Ray's eyes flashed from one hand to the other in confusion. He let Riley go and stared at his palms.

Riley didn't waste another second. He bolted for the door. If Ray's powers were weaker, maybe the chains were too. He pushed against the metal surface and his hands disappeared to the other side. Riley could feel the wind blowing against his skin.

He threw his shoulder against the door and felt a little resistance but managed to slide through. Ray seized his other arm. Riley strained against the pinching grip, so close to escaping. But with his other hand, Ray made a motion like he was wrenching on a chain. The old man Riley had sent to visit Hazel appeared at the end of the chain. He fell to his knees, a look of terror on his face as his eyes swivelled from Ray to

Riley.

"No!" Riley cried. "Leave him alone!"

Ray dragged Riley back into the bed of the truck, his smile fixed on Riley's face. Riley surrendered, feeling the outside world slip away as his fingertips left the wind behind.

Ray yanked on the chain again and forced the old man to stand face-to-face with the shadow. Ray opened his mouth wide and inhaled.

"No!" Riley screamed as the man's features blurred.

He grabbed Ray's arm and tried to pull him away from the ghost, but Ray barely swayed no matter how hard Riley pulled. In seconds, it was over. The mustached ghost was gone. With an elbow to the chest, Ray sent Riley crashing into the very solid wall, knocking the wind out of him.

Cold guilt froze Riley's stomach as he struggled to pull in a breath. The man was dead because Riley had drawn him into this for help. Riley had put him at risk, and now he was gone forever. His throat tightened, making it even harder to breathe. Was Hazel dead because of him too?

"*Mmm*," Ray's voice hummed over him.

His face looked tranquil and smooth, like he was enjoying something delicious. He smiled down at Riley. Riley buried his face in his knees as he gasped for air, trying to convince himself that Hazel, at least, was fine.

Ray grabbed his chin and forced Riley to meet his eyes, denying him the false privacy.

"Two dead because of you," he said. "Shall we add your mom to the list? Or would you rather tell me your friends' names now?"

"I've told you," Riley choked out. "I don't know anyone else who ... who can see ghosts." He almost stumbled over his words as he realized he also knew Kelly.

"Mom it is, then," Ray smiled. He paused for a long time, waiting for Riley to crack.

Riley thought fast. Kelly had said she fought off a shadow. His mom had no protection, but maybe Kelly could finish Ray. And if he was lucky, Riley might even be able to warn her.

"Kelly," he mumbled at last, feeling like a traitor. "But she's on the other side."

Ray's eyes darted back and forth between Riley's. "The Guardian," he growled.

"You know her," Riley realized.

Then everything made sense. Ray had said the shadow was coming back through a door. This shadow was flitting between both worlds. It was using Ray, a medium, to access the other side. But why?

"Tell me what you know about this Kelly."

22

Chapter 22: Kelly

"Get off me!" Kelly roared, ripping her arm out of Logan's grasp.

She turned back to the door in the middle of the graveyard, but it was gone. All that was left were shadowy headstones and the wind rattling through the branches of the trees.

"No!" she wailed.

She ran across the top of the hill, as if the door might have moved out of sight. The rolling hill was as deserted as before. Kelly rounded on Logan.

"Why did you do that?" she yelled down at him, her voice ragged. "You killed her!"

"No—" Logan insisted, but Kelly didn't let him finish.

"I trusted you!"

"The door was closing—"

"We came here to help her and you—you—"

"She's not dead!" Logan yelled back. "Her soul didn't come through. There were no colours, no ghost, nothing!"

Kelly stared at him with her mouth still open. This truth

settled on her like a blanket.

Logan lowered his voice and took a step up the hill towards her. "She's not dead. But I thought you might be if the shadow closed the door. You'd be trapped as a ghost on the other side. It would *take* you."

Kelly shut her mouth and turned her back on him, scanning the hills for her sister, or the door, or the man, as her thoughts reassembled. Her breath was still coming out in fast plumes on the cold air. Logan was right about one thing: Hazel must still be alive. But that didn't mean she wasn't in danger. And Logan had stopped Kelly from helping her.

She whirled around, worry and anger getting the better of her, and she blasted Logan with a wave of energy, just like at the pool. The explosion knocked him off his feet and he flew through the air, landing with a thud on his back. A sob escaped Kelly as instant guilt mingled with her rage. The familiar exhaustion of using this new power dragged at her limbs. She dropped to her knees and pressed her face to her thighs, letting her hair curtain her from Logan's accusing glare.

But the glare never came. A minute later, she felt Logan's hand on her back as he knelt beside her. She looked up at him with wet eyes. He didn't say a word, only pulled her into a hug. She cried into his shoulder, relieved that he could read her guilt without even having to say a word, that she was allowed to be angry with him at the same time as sorry. That she would still be loved even if he was upset with her too. She had never felt so accepted in all her life, and it made her shake more than ever.

When she had pulled herself together, Logan offered his hand to help her rise. "Next time, make sure there's a pool behind me."

Kelly laughed in spite of herself. She wiped away her tears

and fell quiet as she looked over her shoulder to where the door used to be.

"She'd be here if she were dead," Logan reassured her.

Kelly nodded, then realized he hadn't let go of her hand.

"Come on," he said, giving it a little squeeze. "There's nothing we can do from this side. But maybe you can talk to that boy again."

Kelly allowed him to lead her down the slope and out of the graveyard.

***

Kelly's feet were dragging. She felt drained and worried, and by the time they reached the pond outside the library, her legs felt heavy. She steered Logan towards the brick ledge by the water.

"I just need a minute," she panted, sitting down.

Logan sat next to her, his eyes scanning across the pond to the trees on the far side. The water fountain tinkled in the middle of the pond.

"She saw me," Kelly said. "Hazel. I'm sure of it."

Logan smiled into the distance.

"I wonder why her door was purple."

Logan frowned at that. "Purple?"

"Yeah. The others are always blue."

"It—it looked blue to me," Logan said, looking at her like she'd hit her head.

Kelly squinted at him. "You're not colour-blind, are you?"

Logan laughed. "No, I swear. Did it really look purple to you?"

"Very," Kelly promised. "It was purple the day I went through it too. What colour was yours?"

Logan shrugged. "I don't know, actually. I just remember

walking around here, trying to find people ..."

"Hmm," she said, turning to view the lily pads that were browning with the season and beginning to sink. Between the circles, the moonlight reflected on the black water. "And ... why did the doorframe start to splinter? The others just shut after a soul came through ... They disappeared, but they didn't crack." She twisted to look at the library as she realized she was wrong. "Except that door."

Logan rubbed his chin thoughtfully. "Maybe the doors crack or whatever when a shadow gets someone's ghost. You said it was a shadow after Hazel, right? So the door *started* to crack, but then she got away." He suddenly dropped his voice to a whisper. "I don't mean to scare you but ... I think we're being watched."

Kelly stiffened. "The shadow?"

"I think so," Logan replied, staring in the wrong direction. "Don't look, but I saw something move over by the trees."

"Do you think it's the same one that attacked Hazel?" Kelly whispered back, trying to see out of the very corner of her eye.

"I can't tell," Logan whispered. "But there probably aren't a bunch of them running around here."

Kelly shivered at the very idea. "I think we should go. Before it notices ghosts coming to the library."

Logan jumped to his feet as he realized the importance of what she was saying. "We need to lead it away."

"Back to my house," Kelly suggested, "since it's already compromised. Then maybe we can lose it again."

They strode into the air as casually as they could manage. Kelly struggled to keep her face forwards as they travelled in the middle of the street. Now that Logan had pointed it out, she could feel the shadow's eyes watching her, and the back of her neck prickled.

When she saw her duplex in the distance, Kelly yearned to run for the safety of home, but she knew the walls wouldn't do much good. Even lavender hadn't kept the original Shadow away.

"This shadow is different," Kelly whispered as they drew closer to the house. "The last one tormented us even when it could have taken me. It fed on fear, so it wanted us to be afraid. But this one ... it seems like it's observing us."

"It said you weren't supposed to be here. Maybe it's trying to understand what you are." Logan chanced a glance over his shoulder. "Me, on the other hand ... if I'm not with you, I'm toast."

The memory of the shadow inhaling Logan's colours towards its pit of a mouth made the colour slip from Kelly's face. That had been too close.

They entered through the front door. As soon as they were in the hallway, Kelly said, "I don't like not being able to see it."

Logan strode to the window over the kitchen sink and peered out between the blinds.

"Logan, don't!" Kelly hissed.

"There are no lights on and I'm not touching the blinds," he pointed out.

"*Do* you see it?" Kelly asked, unable to help herself as she twisted and untwisted her fingers.

He shook his head. "No, but it's out there somewhere."

Kelly looked up as if she could see through the ceiling. "What if it gets in the house and starts listening to us?"

"We should leave before it gets the chance," Logan agreed. "But we need to know where it is so we don't run right into it."

Kelly's shoulders were up by her ears she was so tense. "I'll check the backyard. Stay out of sight!"

Kelly swept off down the hall as soft and swift as a ghost. Her heart almost gave out at the sight of the exposed sliding glass door. The shadow had first appeared there. She snuck in from the side to peer out. A tall fence shadowed the short backyard, separating Kelly's house from the back neighbour's. She eyed the corners of the fence, where the darkest shadows lurked. Her mind tried to show her faces in the knots of wood.

"Anything?" Logan called, making her flinch.

"Nothing," she returned.

A glass-shattering scream sounded outside. Kelly clutched the back of an armchair for support as all the breath left her body. Logan raced into the living room to see if she had screamed. He grabbed her elbow like Kelly might faint, and if she had a body, she might have.

Kelly could hear Logan breathing in the silence that followed. When the scream came again, they both jumped.

"Sounds like a banshee," Logan whispered, his grip on Kelly's elbow painful.

She didn't answer. She knew that voice but didn't want to believe her ears.

"Kelly!" the voice screamed in agony.

"No," Logan said immediately, pulling Kelly around so that she faced him. "It's trying to lure you out."

Kelly turned towards the continued scream, but Logan grabbed her chin and locked eyes.

"Whoever that is, it's not really them."

"But it could be," Kelly insisted, her lower lip trembling. "That man who attacked Hazel ... He could have gotten her."

Logan shook his head and squeezed her shoulders. "It's too much of a coincidence."

"But this is our old house," Kelly went on, even as she hoped he would talk her out of it. "She *would* come here."

The scream cut through their whispered conversation: "Kelly, help me!"

"We should run," Logan said, "in the opposite direction. It'll expect you out that way. This is our chance."

Kelly hesitated, but Logan said, "Trust me."

She let him pull her to the kitchen, but the continued screams caused a cold sweat to break out across her body. Logan peered through the front window.

"I don't see anything. Let's go."

He disappeared through the kitchen cupboards and out into the front yard. Kelly followed. The night air pushed the hair away from her face as Logan sprinted across the grass. She followed, but the screams kept calling her, and her concern for Hazel slowed her feet. She had to see for herself.

Kelly forced herself as far as the house across the street, but then she crouched beside the neighbour's car.

"What are you doing?" Logan whispered from the opposite side of the house, where he was about to slip into the backyard.

Kelly raised a finger to mime 'just one second' as she crept around the back of the car. She squinted around the side to get a look at her own side-yard. Her breath abandoned her.

Hazel was on her knees with the shadow standing over her. Its unhinged jaw was gaping wide as it sucked in a deep breath. Colours began slipping from Hazel towards its dark mouth.

"No!" Kelly croaked, her voice little more than vapour on the cold air. "Hazel!"

She leapt to her feet and slammed her hands against the air, hoping it would work from this distance. A wave of energy rippled out across the night sky. It stormed across the street towards the shadow like an upright sheet of glass. Its speed and power sucked Kelly forwards another step.

The energy went straight through the two figures on the lawn, and they disintegrated into black smoke. Kelly's breath caught in her throat. In a second both Hazel and the shadow were gone, and the sheet of energy flickered out in the distance. Kelly's hands dropped. The silence on the street was deafening as she searched for the shadow.

She glanced back towards Logan, who waved her over, his mouth a tense line. Kelly retreated. When he saw she was coming, he slipped through the gap beside the neighbour's house. Kelly rounded the corner after him, her eyes still scanning the street.

"Your guilt for your sister is delicious," a deep voice said.

Kelly skidded to a halt. The shadow had Logan trapped in its arms, a smoky hand covering his mouth; a shadow restraining a ghost. Its eyes were locked on Kelly's. It was like being in death's spotlight. Her thoughts raced, a blur of discarded ideas. She had used up too much energy on the vision of Hazel, and the shadow knew it.

"Poor Kelly," it said with obvious relish, "afraid of her own shadow. Unable to save anyone."

Kelly tried to raise her hands to call up more energy, but her arms wouldn't respond. She was frozen with fear. The shadow squeezed Logan tighter as if embracing him, smiling. Even with half his face covered, Logan looked repulsed.

Then it loosened its other hand and made a gesture as if asking Kelly to rise. Black shadows followed its hand instead, rising from the ground in spikes that flickered and darted. Black fire. A line of flames separated Kelly from Logan, growing until they towered over Kelly. She stumbled back as the heat engulfed her, tingling like electricity.

Her eyes flashed back to the shadow. Logan was struggling to pull away as the shadow turned his face head-on, its jaw unhinging.

"Logan!" Kelly screamed.

The shadow inhaled. Kelly raised her hands with a groan, sweat trickling down her brow. Colours stretched from Logan's face into the air. Kelly cried out with effort as she slammed her palms against the air, but it was like pushing her hands through a blanket rather than glass. The flames flickered as the wobbling blow met their defending line. Kelly's efforts were wasted. The fire absorbed the energy and rushed her. She tripped backwards and fell.

The flames latched onto her foot, disintegrating her shoe into smoke. Black lines crawled up her calf as if her veins were turning black. Kelly screamed in agony and rolled across the grass, away from the fire. She swiped at her calf and foot to stifle the burns.

She limped back up, teeth gritted against the pulsing pain. Through the flickering black flames, she saw the shadow glowering at Logan, the colours gone.

"Your soul is tainted," it spat. "You are useless to me." Its eyes swivelled to Kelly. "But perhaps the Guardian would like to know who you really are."

The shadow strode through the fire without even a flinch, dragging Logan in a headlock. Kelly staggered back.

"This," the shadow said, crushing Logan in its grip so that he gasped for air, "is what's left of my kin after your kind destroyed it. The soul core."

Kelly stared from the shadow to Logan, uncomprehending.

"He is here," the shadow said, tipping its head to an unnatural angle, "because he cannot go on. He is not whole. But why are you here, Kelly Connors?"

Kelly's breath hitched. How did it know her name?

"Perhaps I will see what can be salvaged of my kind," the shadow said. It looked down at Logan from the strange angle. "I doubt your friend will like it."

The shadow burst into a blur of smoke that obscured Logan.

"Leave now, Guardian," its eery voice called. "Next I come for you."

It slipped into the nearest shadow—the trees next to the house—and blended away until Kelly was looking at nothing but an empty, starlit neighbourhood. The flames were gone. Logan and the shadow were gone. Kelly stared at her empty palms. Hope drained away like her powers.

23

Chapter 23: Hazel

"I don't want to go home," Hazel insisted. "If this man is watching me, it puts everyone at risk. Can't I stay at a hotel for the night?"

Riva's dad sighed as he turned the steering wheel, continuing their journey home from the police station. It was 4:30 in the morning and the streets were still empty.

"You're safer with people around. I want to keep an eye on you."

"But—"

"Cops will be patrolling the neighbourhood for this guy, and *I'll* be sleeping on the couch," he said, as if confident that he would be the deciding factor of her safety. "I'll sleep there until they catch him if I have to."

Hazel fell silent, rather touched by Jermaine's vow.

"Same," Derrick piped up from the back.

Hazel twisted around in her seat to smile at her brother, whose chin was set. "I appreciate that. But I promised your sister I'd look out for you. Staying with me right now ..."

"He's coming too," Jermaine countered.

Derrick gave her a smug grin.

"We care about you, Hazel." Jermaine gave her a knowing look that Derrick couldn't see. "Would I bring him with me, if I wasn't sure everything would be okay?"

Hazel settled back into her seat. She still felt jittery, but warmth calmed her heart at his words. She couldn't remember the last time an adult had told her everything would be okay. She savoured the sound.

When they arrived at the house, Jermaine pulled a baseball bat from the trunk. None of them commented on it. Hazel set her keys down as quietly as she could on the kitchen counter, then retrieved some spare blankets from the closet upstairs.

Downstairs, Jermaine took them off Hazel's hands and pulled her into a tight hug.

"Get some sleep," he whispered over her shoulder. "You're safe now."

They barely had time to separate before Derrick took Jermaine's place. Hazel chuckled. She had missed these two, living on her own.

"Goodnight," she whispered. "Thank you."

Before she went back upstairs, Hazel retrieved the note she had left on the kitchen table, glad the girls hadn't seen it and worried. The same warmth she felt earlier flooded her chest. This time power surged down her arms and made her hands tremble until she crumpled the paper in her fist. She frowned, unsure what to make of it. Then she chalked it up to leftover adrenaline and went up to bed.

***

Sunlight was streaming across her bed when Hazel woke the next morning. The bed beside her was empty. Hazel stretched and rose to pull her warm housecoat off the back of the door.

She emerged into the hall at the same time as Kate.

"Well, good morning," Kate said, folding her arms. "Imagine my surprise when I went to watch TV at breakfast, only to find a man sleeping on the couch."

Hazel laughed. "Sorry, Kate. We didn't want to wake everyone last night."

"Never mind that," Kate said with a wave of her hand. "We're dying to hear everything."

Kate dragged Hazel downstairs where they found Jermaine at the table, scrolling on his phone while Riva did homework across from him. Derrick and Jen were on the couch. The girls usually had a later start on Saturdays. Jen leapt to her feet when she saw Hazel coming down the stairs.

"Jermaine told us what happened," Jen said, throwing her arms around Hazel's neck. "I can't believe it. Don't ever go out alone in the middle of the night again."

"Never?" Hazel teased.

Jen gave her a teary 'Don't joke about this' look.

Hazel pulled Jen back into the hug and said gently, "I'm fine."

They joined the others at the table, and Hazel went through the events of last night yet again. She ate her toast while the others peppered her with questions.

"Two things are bothering me," Hazel said at last. "One thing he said was 'My meals keep getting away. I have to close the doors.'" She frowned at the crumbs on her plate, seeing the graveyard in their stead. "There was a door when he was choking me. I saw it. It was breaking. And ... I saw Kelly."

She looked up at the rapt expressions on everyone's faces and knew they were thinking what she was: She had either seen a glimpse of the afterlife through that door, or she had hallucinated. Jen's hand twitched next to Hazel's.

"So he wants to close all the doors ..." Riva broke the silence. "That implies that he attacked you and Riley because mediums have access to these doors."

"It makes sense," Jen said, nodding. "You've always been able to see things we can't, and you help ghosts move on. Maybe they go through these doors."

"And he wants to close them because he can't get the ghosts once they're on the other side!" Kate said, slapping her hands on the table. "He's like a medium serial killer!"

"Okay, okay," Jermaine said, raising his hand in a 'settle down' gesture. "Let's not scare ourselves without proof."

"What's the other thing that's bothering you?" Derrick asked from where he was leaning against the wall.

Hazel swallowed, her throat suddenly tight. "He said maybe I would see Riley on the other side."

There was the briefest pause, then everyone chimed in with words of reassurance.

"But what if he's not okay? What if his soul is gone?" Hazel's voice cracked. "How do I tell his mom?"

"You don't," Jermaine said. "If you give me her number, I'll tell her what happened and your concern. But the main thing to remember is this man was probably lying to upset you. There's hope." He reached over and clapped Hazel's shoulder.

Hazel managed a weak smile.

"So," Jermaine went on, "how are you feeling now that it's daytime? Do you want to stay here for the day, or come home with us?"

"Mom and I were going to repaint our old bedroom," Riva offered. "Make it more mature, like a spare room. You could help?"

Hazel shook her head. "I don't want to put your family in

danger. I think it's best if I stay here. But I—I don't want to stay alone."

"I could stay," Riva offered. "I'm sure Mom wouldn't mind rescheduling, considering."

"No," Hazel said. "Don't change your plans because of me. I'll be fine."

"I'll be home today," Kate said. "So you won't be alone."

"I'll call in sick," Jen added.

Hazel smiled truly at that. The same feeling of warmth that spread down her arms last night rolled through her again.

Riva opened her mouth like she was about to say something more, but then she rose from the table. Her action closed the unofficial breakfast meeting.

"Perfect," Jermaine said, also rising. "I'll come back and stay the night again, just to be sure. And make sure you keep the doors locked today. Make smart decisions."

Hazel, Jen, and Kate nodded. Hazel gave Elisabeth's number to Jermaine, said goodbye to him and Derrick, then went upstairs to dress. She ran into Riva in the hallway.

"Have fun at your mom's," Hazel said.

"Mhm," Riva replied as she continued to the stairs.

"What's wrong?" Hazel asked with concern.

Riva paused with one hand on the railing. When she looked back at Hazel, her eyes were shining with tears. "You told me not to change my plans for you, then you let Jen change hers. I thought when we moved in together, everything would go back to the way it was, but you spend all your time with her. You never come back to visit my family, but you go for dinner with hers. It feels like you're done with us. Like you don't need me anymore."

A tear spilled from Riva's eye, but she brushed it away

before rushing down the stairs, leaving Hazel at the top, dumb-founded.

"Riva! It's not like that; it's—"

But Riva slipped past the occupied girls and guests downstairs and disappeared out the front door. Hazel remained where she was, one hand on the railing as her stomach sank and sank.

Hadn't she just called on Riva's family for help? Clearly, she wasn't done with them. It was true she had been spending time with Jen's family, but she had moved in with their daughter. Plus, Riva was working part-time and both she and Hazel were in school. Yet they had just managed a get-together with all their old friends. And they *lived* together. Hazel frowned. What more could Riva expect of her?

Even as she thought it, guilt twisted Hazel's stomach. There was something in the way Riva said, 'You don't need me anymore' that sounded a lot like 'You don't want me anymore.' Tears stung Hazel's eyes. She never fought with Riva, and she had never meant to make her feel neglected. She hated this feeling.

Jen appeared at the bottom of the stairs. "Hey," she said. "Can we chat?"

Hazel's heart sank even further. This didn't sound like a normal chat. She led the way to their bedroom and closed the door behind Jen.

"I can't help but be upset with you," Jen said, sitting down on the edge of the bed. "I'm really glad you're safe, but you went out alone in the middle of the night to a secluded area where you were vulnerable. And you didn't even tell me. And look what happened!"

Frustration rose in Hazel's throat. "I know," she said, "but I didn't know I was going to a cemetery, and I thought I was just picking up Riley. *And* I left a note!"

Jen raised her palms in self-defence. "I didn't see any note, but—"

"I didn't want to wake you!" Hazel went on, hackles rising. "I thought I was being *nice*."

"I'd rather you wake me if you're about to disappear," Jen said with an arched eyebrow. "Better safe than—"

Hazel interrupted again. "Look, I'm alive, okay? And besides, it's a little safer for me to be out in the night than you."

Jen's eyes narrowed. "What's that supposed to mean?"

"I have training I can rely on," Hazel said, thumbing her chest. "And I'm bigger than you, okay? I'm more intimidating as a target—"

"Okay," Jen said pointedly as she stood up, "let's not exaggerate things here. You almost died, remember?"

"I'm just saying, I couldn't have predicted this!"

"And I'm just saying, next time, wake me up!" Jen said, her voice rising. She gave Hazel an incredulous look and stalked out of the room.

Hazel shut her eyes for a moment. She knew Jen was right, and that she had reacted poorly because of the rapid onslaught of accusations. Hazel strode over to her bed and collapsed backwards on the mattress. She ran her hands over her face and reminded herself that she had more pressing things to deal with.

***

Riva and Jermaine had not yet returned as the sun set for the evening. Hazel had spent the day in a haze of homework and naps in her bedroom. Her throat was sore from the man's hands around her neck, and she was exhausted from arguing with people she loved. With a sigh, Hazel rose from her desk and pulled back the bedroom curtain. The ghost woman was standing on the front lawn again, looking over her shoulders.

Hazel chewed her lip for a moment. The woman was tied to the shadow. It was time to hear what she had to say. Hazel tapped on the glass and the woman looked up. Her face lit up with hope. Hazel jerked her head towards the back of the house. She would talk to her in the backyard.

She let the curtain drop. Reaching for the lavender necklace to remove it, Hazel came up empty-handed. She had already lost it in the graveyard. She slipped out of her room and tiptoed down the stairs. Jen was cooking in the kitchen, so Hazel was able to round the corner unnoticed. She passed through the narrow hallway to the laundry room, and unlocked the backdoor.

Cold air blew into the house, and Hazel shivered. She strained to see across the small grassy backyard. Then, at the bottom of the three steps, the woman appeared.

"At last," she said with a smile of relief.

Hazel gave her a tight-lipped smile in return, unwilling to apologize.

"There's someone you need to talk to," the woman said, and she indicated to the corner of the house.

Hazel squinted against the dark. At first, she saw no one. Then, out from around the corner stepped the man who had tried to kill her.

24

Chapter 24: Riley

"Ray," Riley said, shaking the man's shoulder. "Please, wake up!"

Sirens blared in the distance. If they didn't move soon, the police would find them. Ray would be arrested, and the shadow would come back for Sasha. Riley would be stuck in this truck for endless cycles of days and nights until someone pulled the plug on his body at the hospital.

"Wake up, sweetheart," Sasha said, trying and failing to push back Ray's hair. "Come on, Ray, we need you."

The man stirred, rolling his head to the side on the hard truck bed.

"That's it," she encouraged. "Come back to us."

At last, Ray's eyes opened. The lines on his face smoothed out as his eyes settled on Sasha's face. He smiled. She smiled back. He raised a hand to touch her cheek, but it only met air. His serene expression shattered, and he squeezed his eyes shut as Riley watched his heart break all over again.

"We need your help, Ray," Sasha said. "Quickly, while the shadow's gone. It's time to let me go."

"No." Ray's voice was a rasp. "I can't live without you. I can't."

"This isn't living anyway," Sasha said. She stroked his cheek without ever touching it. "And that shadow's not going to let me go. I think you know this."

"I'll protect you," Ray whispered.

Sasha shook her head, her eyes wet with tears. "I know you would if you could. But you can't. Please let me go."

"We were supposed to get old," Ray choked, a tear rolling toward his ear. "If I'd just turned faster—"

"Don't say that," Sasha cut him off. "It was an accident. Accidents happen all the time. There was nothing you could have done. I forgave you, Ray. I forgave you right away. Why won't you hear me?"

"I can never forgive myself," Ray whispered. When he squeezed his eyes shut again, tears fell.

Sasha met Riley's gaze. "Then make it right."

"Ray," Riley said, "the shadow's gone after my friend on the other side. Let Sasha warn her. Help us save her."

"And yourself," Sasha added in a whisper. "Open the door. Do it for both of us."

Ray sat up, swiping the tears away from his face and running his fingers through his hair. He took a deep breath, but his composure cracked again when he looked at Sasha.

"Please don't leave me."

Sasha bowed her head in misery. Riley's heart ached for the man who had imprisoned him. He knew all too well what it was like to be left behind.

"My dad was taken by a shadow," Riley said. A muscle worked in his chin as he struggled to keep himself composed. "You have no idea what I'd give to get to say goodbye."

Sasha nodded, her hands hovering over Ray's. "He's right. We are so lucky."

Ray managed a weak smile as he looked into his wife's eyes. "I had no idea how lucky I was. I thought I did, but ..."

A small sob escaped Sasha. She choked out, "I feel the same way. And if we can be together again someday, we will. Even if it's in another life. Trust me."

Ray let out a shaking breath and closed his eyes again. A blue light illuminated the three figures huddled in the back of the truck. In the side wall, a door appeared. Through that portal Riley could see a matching deserted road and a forest of trees beyond.

Ray rose to his knees and tried in vain to take Sasha's hand. "Let me come with you," he begged. "My life here is over without you. I *never* wanted to live without you. But now I've done terrible things." Another siren in the distance seemed to punctuate his point. "It doesn't have to end like this. Let's go together."

Sasha glanced at Riley as she wiped away her falling tears. Riley could practically feel the ache in her chest as his own. "No, Ray," she said in a whisper. "You have to make this right first. You owe it to Riley."

Ray bowed his head.

"I love you," Sasha said, placing her forehead to his as if she could feel it.

He opened his eyes and stared into hers, love and pain passing between them. She smiled her understanding, her tears falling freely now.

"I have to go now," she said. "Before it's too late."

She got to her feet as if a heavy weight were on her shoulders, then approached the door. She turned to Riley and said, "I'll do what I can."

Riley nodded his gratitude. "Be safe."

With one last look, Sasha said, "Ray. Thank you." Then she stepped through the door.

She didn't fall to the ground. Her body turned to a rainbow of colours that swirled in the wind. It carried her into the forest of trees. Then she was gone. The blue glow continued as Riley stared out into the other world, but the truck somehow seemed darker.

After a long silence, Riley looked at Ray through the corner of his eye. He was staring at the ground, his shoulder slumped in utter defeat. Riley chewed the inside of his cheek, afraid to speak, but equally afraid of the shadow's return.

He cleared his throat. The shadow had never been gone this long before. "Thank you, Ray," he began, echoing Sasha.

Ray didn't move. Riley took a hesitant step closer. "How do we get out of here?"

Ray shook his head almost imperceptibly from side to side, like he was testing to see if he could still move. Then his hand rose to the chain around his neck and he pulled out the empty jar. "You can only leave the chains with a false body."

Riley's heart sank.

Ray looked up at him with a heavy sigh. "You can take mine."

"What do you mean?"

"In the jar or not, the police will be after me," Ray went on, "but if they get me, you're better off in a body than in the jar."

"You want me to possess you?" Riley asked, his eyebrows rising in disbelief. "Is that possible?"

Ray shrugged. "I don't—I don't want to be here anymore. I don't care anymore. But Sasha—" his voice cracked on her name "—it's what she would want. So go on. You have my permission."

"But ... how do I do it?"

Ray held out his hand, palm up. Riley gnawed his cheek a moment longer, the spot feeling raw, then placed his hand on top. It sunk an inch into Ray's hand. The moment it did, it was like magnets were pulling their hands together. Suddenly Riley could feel Ray's hand like it was his own. The magnetic feeling intensified. Then, just like with the jar, Riley was gone. He looked down at his hands, which were no longer his.

"Ray?" he asked the empty truck. His new voice startled him.

Ray didn't respond and Riley didn't waste any more time. He rushed to the rolling back door of the truck and seized the handle. The feel of the solid handle under his fingers was a relief. He threw the door open. The sunlight outside blinded him. The sky was a bright winter blue, and the wind bit. He leapt down to the street and stared up and down its length. He had no idea where he was.

"Do I ... leave you now?" Riley asked.

The only response Riley got was a tight feeling of panic in his chest. It could only mean two things: Either Ray did not want to be alone, or Riley would die this far from his body.

The risk was too uncertain. Riley reached into his pocket and found Ray's phone. He didn't dare call anyone in case the police had identified Ray and flagged it. The phone needed a swiping pattern for entry, and Ray's fingers did the job without Riley's help.

"Thank you," he said.

He tapped the app icon and found a recently opened map with a red dot.

"Is that Hazel's house?"

Riley couldn't hear Ray's answer, but he could feel the yes.

"And where are we?"

Ray's fingers slid the map until it showed a side road on the other side of town. By the looks of it, Hazel's house was pretty far away. He couldn't walk that distance, and he didn't know how much time Kelly had. He pulled himself into the driver's seat. A stranger's hands gripped the cold steering wheel. Riley stared at the fogged-up windshield. There was no way the police weren't looking for Ray's truck.

A cord extending from Riley's chest lit up. Riley started in surprise. Ray was calling to someone. The cord extended out to the road, where a woman appeared. She had blonde hair, a curvy figure, and a look of terror on her face at the sight of them. Riley scrambled out of the truck, placating her with his raised palms.

"I'm not the shadow," he called. "I'm not Ray, either. I'm Riley. Well, Ray is here, but I'm Riley. And I need your help."

The woman gave him a scathing look.

Riley cleared his throat and plunged on, "I have to get to my friend Hazel. Her sister is in danger."

"*She's* in danger from you," the woman spat.

Riley shook his head no. "Ray, drop the cord."

Ray obeyed, and the blue light vanished.

"Can you feel the shadow's hooks?" he asked her. "They don't reach out from me."

The woman frowned, but she seemed to test it out. Her face went from glowering to amazement in the space of a second. Her eyes pierced Riley. "Is it ... Is it really gone?"

Riley screwed up his face apologetically. "Well ... no, not really. Temporarily, I think. That's why we have to move fast."

She shook her head. "I can't take you to Hazel. If the shadow could come back at any time, I'd be putting her in danger. We would *all* be in danger. Besides, she won't see me. I've been trying to reach her for days."

"You have?" Riley asked.

The woman's expression went cold again as she looked Riley up and down. "Ray here killed my friend. She was a medium, just like him. They all were."

Riley tried not to take her disgusted look personally. "Who are 'they?' "

"Ray's friends, or so he had us believe," she said, her voice icy. "The mediums he met online. He tracked them down for this shadow. They tried to warn Hazel, but with the shadow watching them, they couldn't do much. They had to go into hiding because *Ray* was picking them off one by one, and a connection to her, via cord or online, was something Ray could follow. I was left to warn Hazel."

"They didn't warn *me*," Riley said.

"There were stories around Hazel," the woman said with a shrug. "She was traceable."

Once again, Riley remembered that Hazel had worked as a medium for hire.

"But Ray must have found something on you," the woman went on.

Riley couldn't think of anything public that might point to his ability. He blew past it. "It doesn't matter now," he said with a shake of his head. "Hazel would want to know about her sister. Will you help me?"

The woman crossed her arms. "What exactly do you want from me?"

"I need a guide," Riley said, thinking fast. He indicated his new body. "The police are after Ray, and I have to get all the way across town looking like this. Can you steer me clear of them?"

The woman grimaced. "They'll have put out a public alert about you. There's no telling who we need to avoid."

Riley ran his hands through his hair, starting at the unexpected length of it. He sighed. "I'll have to try."

The woman pressed her lips together, unconvinced.

"Hazel would do anything for her sister," Riley promised. He had never seen the two together, but he knew this was true of Hazel and anyone she cared about. "She would want to know this, no matter the danger."

The woman dropped her arms at last. "If anything happens to her, it's on you."

Riley agreed. He climbed back into the truck and started it up before the woman could change her mind. She broke into a jog to check if the coast was clear, but Riley put his window down to stop her as she passed him. "What's your name?"

"Quin," she said over her shoulder.

Riley turned his attention to the truck as she ran on. He studied the dash, gear shift, and signal lights. He had never driven a truck before. He was still learning to drive his mom's sedan. Legally he wasn't even allowed to operate a vehicle without an adult present.

"I hope you're ready in case I screw up, Ray," Riley said, and he turned the vehicle around, the tires crunching over gravel as he followed Quin.

The first few turns were empty of other drivers, but as they headed towards the neighbourhood, a man crossed the road with his border collie. With a pang, Riley thought of Charlie at home. The dog had no idea why Riley had been gone so long. He pulled down his visor so that his arm hid his face as the pair passed. He saw Quin waiting for him at the corner, so he pulled up beside her.

"There are more cars on this road," she warned him. "Drive fast, but not so recklessly people notice."

She took off again, going much faster as a ghost than Riley could have as a human. He peeled around the corner so fast that the truck spat out gravel. Riley winced as Quin threw him a look.

The road was long, lined on one side by mountain and on the other by farmland. Within 10 minutes of winding road, they were back in sight of the city. Riley's palms grew sweaty on the steering wheel.

Quin appeared in the passenger seat next to him, making Riley jerk the wheel. Ray came to the rescue and corrected it. Quin gave him another stern look.

"This area always has some police presence. I think your best bet is to cut through the neighbourhoods on the left. Then we can duck down side streets if need be."

"Got it," Riley breathed, and Quin disappeared again.

Eventually they made it into the centre of town. Here, the traffic had them stopping at every red light, where they were surrounded by cars. Riley's mouth was so dry he could barely swallow. He kept his hands at 10 and two, his face staring straight ahead to avoid eye contact.

Quin appeared beside him again. Riley managed only to flinch.

"We have to get out of here quick," she said. "There's a police car at the next light, going the same direction as us. You'll have to get on the highway and take the next exit."

Sweat began beading on Riley's forehead. "I've never driven on the highway before," he mumbled.

He came from a small town. Even this much traffic was nerve

wracking.

"It's too risky to keep going this way," Quin said.

Riley wet his lips and nodded, thinking to Ray, "Be ready."

Quin directed him to the on-ramp, then went on ahead. Riley stomped on the gas to get up to 100. The truck revved like a jet engine. Feeling shaky as he shoulder-checked, Riley slipped behind a passing car and merged onto the highway.

"This is fine," he said to himself, his voice a little higher than usual. "I'm doing it. This is fine."

He took the next exit and stopped at the light on the overpass. A small giggle escaped him. Ray hadn't even needed to take over.

He went left and found, to his relief, that the road was long, straight, and not too busy. They were nearing farmland again. Quin returned to direct him a few times, but as they approached an intersection, she came back with a grim expression.

"There's police ahead. A roadblock."

"What?" Riley gasped.

"I think someone reported you."

"What do I do? Turn around?" Riley did a jerky shoulder-check as if he was about to do a U-turn here and now.

Quin patted his shoulder to steady him, but neither of them could feel it. "They'll be patrolling everywhere. I think you need to abandon the truck."

Riley swore. "But if they find it, they'll start searching for me, and I can't get far on foot."

Quin made a clicking noise with her tongue and said, "You have no choice."

Riley scanned the roadsides, but there was nowhere to hide the truck. Now he was really sweating.

"There's a school up ahead," Quin said. "It's a bit close to the roadblock, but maybe you can park behind it."

Riley's throat started to close up and he thought he might be having a panic attack. If he was caught, would he be stuck in this body and go to jail? He couldn't seem to catch his breath. Or could he abandon Ray to life in jail and somehow get back to his own body? What if he couldn't? Was he basically dead?

"There it is," Quin said, pointing at the school. "Drive casually now."

Swallowing with difficulty, Riley signalled left and waited for a gap in traffic as cars lined up behind him. He peered ahead. He saw an officer directing traffic. He wiped his brow.

He made the left and prayed people would think he was a maintenance worker. He looped behind the school and parked out of sight.

"You're not out of the woods yet," Quin reminded him.

But Riley leapt out of the truck and felt better when his feet hit the ground. He shut the door of the truck behind him and hoped to never see it again.

"Over the fence?" he asked Quin, eyeing up the chain-link. It was covered in blackberry thorns.

"The fastest route to Hazel's is straight across the farms. But it will be hard to hide."

Riley nodded and squared his nerves. He picked a spot in the fence with minimal brambles and took a running leap. The fence shook and rattled as he made his way over.

"Ouch," he said on the other side, rubbing his shoulder. Ray didn't have the same agility Riley did.

He crouched among the blackberries as Quin went on ahead. She reappeared a moment later.

"There's a creek that dips down a bit. If you can get there fast, you can hide."

Riley nodded once and bolted across the open field. The day was cold enough that most of the mud was frozen solid, making it easier to navigate. Short spikes of golden grass stabbed the air where they were cut, crunching underfoot. Riley didn't dare look over his shoulder towards the roadblock. He left that to Quin. The wind bit his ears, and Ray's muscles strained.

At last, Riley reached the ridge of the creek and skidded down towards the murky water. He kept his head ducked low as he clutched his side, wheezing. Ray was too tall to be fully hidden.

"Okay," Quin said, arriving at the top of the ridge. "I think you're clear. But if I were you, I would backtrack to those farmhouses. It will look like you live there and are out working."

"Or the owners will see me and call the cops," Riley countered.

"The field is too open," Quin warned.

Riley rubbed his eyes. "Fine."

He spent so much time ducking behind trees or stooping to pretend to fix a fence that an hour went by before Riley made it to the next road. He was at the edge of the city now, and finally on Hazel's side of town. He jogged across the road and made it into the neighbourhood beyond, out of sight of the general traffic, and well beyond the police roadblock. Riley swiped at his brow again and let out a sigh of relief.

"Don't stop now," Quin cautioned. "You've got to make up time."

Riley rested his hands on his knees and groaned. This was going to be a long, awful day.

25

Chapter 25: Kelly

Kelly kicked the wall of the pool where the boy, Riley, had not reappeared. The sky was turning grey through the skylight as dawn approached. No matter what Kelly did, the wall stayed white and blank. She supposed it was him who had opened the door in the first place, not her. A Traveller, not a Guardian.

She scoffed at the word 'Guardian.' She couldn't even protect a shoe. She glanced down at her burned toes, then did a doubletake. Her shoe was whole again. She dropped to the hard floor and pulled it off, examining every inch. Then she pulled off her sock. The tops of her toes were still singed, black and tender, but her sock and shoe were completely intact. She stared for a long moment. An idea occurred to her and she imagined that the sock in her hand was gone. It vanished. She willed it back, and it came.

It was just like when Logan had shown her the tree on day one and how to pat it without sending her hand through. It was a matter of will. She fixed her gaze on the skylight and imagined her foot was smooth and pale again. When she looked back at her foot, the ugly black lines still endured. It seemed that a soul, her essence, could take real damage here. Who knew how long that would take to heal?

She didn't like to think what the shadow might be doing to Logan's soul. She fussed with the laces of her shoes. Where had it taken him? The shadow's words kept circling in her head. Logan was what was left of a shadow after it was destroyed. Did that mean Logan was once a shadow? Is that why he had been stuck here all this time—because a shadow had anchored him to the living world before it, too, died? Kelly shivered at the thought of her head on a shadow's shoulder last night.

"No," she said aloud, jumping up and resuming her pacing.

The shadow was tormenting her like it had with the image of Hazel. That was all.

"Where would it take him?" she asked her echo.

There was only one place the old Shadow would go. Kelly's heart lurched at the very thought. She was happy this was a unique shadow, and she didn't have to return there. But this new shadow had been all over town, from the library to the hospital. Kelly would have to start her search there.

She glared at the wall. "Anytime you want to help, Riley, that would be great."

She strode out of the gym and emerged into the sunlit street only to crash into something solid. Kelly yelped as a woman caught her elbow to stop her from falling. Kelly wrenched herself free and darted back.

"Sorry!" the woman cried. "It's just me."

"You?" Kelly said, taking in the short dark hair and olive skin. The woman wore the same black clothes as yesterday. "You're the ghost who was with Riley."

The woman nodded. "Sasha."

Kelly realized she had one fist up like she was about to block a blow. She lowered her arm. "He let you go? The shadow let you go?"

There was a flicker of sadness in Sasha's eyes. "The shadow doesn't know I'm gone. I came to help you."

Kelly was still leaning away as if on the verge of running. "But," she said, frowning, "how are you here? Ghosts always pass right through."

Sasha smiled at that. "Unlike you, I actually am a Guardian."

Kelly's eyes widened with interest, but she refused to let her guard down. She peppered Sasha with questions. "What is a Guardian? And if I'm not one, then what am I?"

"You know what you are," Sasha said with a small smile. "You're a Medium."

"Why does the shadow think I'm a Guardian then? Why can I ... do what I can do to it? Why can I force it away?"

"This is a conversation we can have while we search," Sasha said. "We have to find this shadow. We have to stop it."

It was too good to be true. Kelly wanted to let this full-grown adult woman take over, to sit back and follow rather than lead. But something inside her tensed against the idea.

"I was thinking of checking the hospital," she said, deciding to put this woman to work as she made up her mind. "I've seen it there before."

"Lead the way."

The two women took off at a run, passing straight through buildings but keeping their feet on the ground.

"How are we going to stop it?" Kelly asked.

Sasha pressed her lips into a tight line for a moment. "I'm hoping you can do that."

Kelly threw her an eyebrow.

Sasha didn't accept the silent disagreement. "A Guardian," she said, "is not as impressive as it sounds. We don't have special weapons or talents. But when we are close to a Medium, things are different. We're the people who say we've seen a ghost out of the corner of our eye. More importantly, we can see other threats. Like shadows. And most importantly, we seem to amplify the power of a Medium."

"Oh," Kelly breathed as they cut across a gas station and weaved between the pumps.

"The shadow thought you were a Guardian because you were protecting a Medium. That's the Guardian's role. They are an extra set of eyes."

"So it thought I was protecting Logan?"

"Who's Logan?" Sasha asked with surprise. "I was thinking of Riley."

Kelly bit her lip before answering. "Logan is my ... my friend. The shadow took him."

"Ah," Sasha said. "I'm so sorry."

"It's fine, we're going to get him back," she vowed. "He's not dead. The shadow couldn't kill him. It said he ... used to be one of them."

Sasha blinked several times fast.

"I don't know what it wants with him," Kelly confessed, unable to keep the worry from showing on her face. "But it didn't sound good."

Sasha stopped running, and Kelly faltered. The woman studied Kelly's expression for a moment, and Kelly saw a kindness there that the shadow could never have faked.

"I've never heard of your ability to attack a shadow," Sasha said, "and I doubt the shadow has either. But with me here, you might be strong enough to stop it. Don't give up yet."

Kelly managed a weak smile. She continued across the street. "So you think it's a Medium thing," she said.

"Mediums are the most powerful sensitives, and Mediumship usually comes with some other secondary power. Like Riley with his Traveller abilities. Maybe this is another subset."

"I don't think I'm very powerful," Kelly said. "Not like my sister."

It was Sasha's turn to throw her a look. "You asked why I didn't float away like the other ghosts? It's because I could feel your presence. It called to me. A Medium to a Guardian. You're more powerful than you realize."

They arrived at the hospital just as Kelly was about to ask what the other subsets of Mediums were. Sasha put a finger to her lips. They slunk inside.

The two searched the hospital from ER to rooftop. It was less disconcerting in the daylight, but Kelly still did not like the unnatural quiet. The shadow was nowhere to be found. Frustrated at wasting so much time with Logan in danger, Kelly led the way back to her house. The shadow wasn't there either. They decided to try the library next, but Kelly was beginning to despair of ever finding it.

Their efforts at the library proved just as fruitless. Kelly collapsed on the edge of the pond where she and Logan had sat last night. She ironed her face with her hands.

"There's no need for that," Sasha said. "But we may have to give up the idea of sneaking up on it. What if we bring it to us instead?"

"But will it bring Logan with it?" Kelly asked.

"If this gets the shadow away from Logan, all the better, don't you think?"

Kelly bounced her leg with nerves. She considered the library.

"We can't do it here."

"Then where?"

"The school," she said, getting to her feet. "I saw it there my first day."

The afternoon was wearing on, and the temperature was growing colder, so the two ran faster to warm up. When they reached the school, Sasha grabbed Kelly's arm.

"It's here," she said, her eyes unfocused as if she could sense the shadow.

Kelly wet her lips and stared up at the hulking grey school. Sasha gave her an encouraging squeeze.

"Let's destroy this thing."

Kelly laughed through her nose. She rolled her shoulders back and led the way inside.

They entered through the front doors of the school. As before, the October leaves skittered down the floor like spiders, leading the way. The lobby gave Kelly the creeps without its usual influx of students. It was better than the last day she had seen them all, she reflected. The pushing. The screaming. She tried to shake off the memories.

Kelly approached the glass window of the office on soft feet and peered into the depths. There were no signs of movement. She pointed with a nod of her chin towards the left, where a hallway passed the gym. They crept along the hall past empty classroom after empty classroom with nothing but desks inside.

Then they reached Kelly's Social Studies room on the right. Goosebumps ran down her arms. There she had sat, in a desk in the middle of the room, trying to hold back her tears at the loss of Gran. Not knowing she was about to experience the worst and last day of her life. In the sunlight, the dark memory seemed to mock her.

"No shadow," Sasha said, having checked the remaining rooms.

Kelly jerked back to the present. "Let's keep going."

They backtracked, passing Kelly's locker. There she had swapped out her binder and textbook one last time. Kelly couldn't help the way her heartbeat sped up as they retraced her old footsteps to the lobby. She sped back past the office, pushing aside the sight of spurting blood and falling students as she went. Sasha hurried along in her wake, oblivious to the haunting images.

But Kelly knew where to go next. As the jostling students panicked, Kelly had pushed her way into the next hall. An announcement had called for lockdown mode, and someone had bumped into her, sending her books tumbling. One of the books went skidding down the hall and disappeared underfoot. Kelly abandoned them.

She remembered Hazel saying she had Math, and Kelly grabbed the backpack of a passing student heading that direction. She let him pull her through the clogged hall. The screaming grew closer and closer behind them. The pushing reached a violent pitch and jerked the strap out of her hand.

She pressed on, a mere doorway from Hazel's class. In the now shadowy, empty hallway, Kelly saw a figure lying facedown on the cold floor. Logan was lying just where she herself had finally fallen.

She raced to his side, sliding a little as she dropped to her knees. She seized his shoulder and rolled him onto his back. He took one look at her and covered his face with his hands, letting out a low moan.

"Logan, what is it?" she asked, clutching one of his wrists like she could save him if she could only hold tight enough.

"I'm so sorry," he choked, his whole body shaking with the whispered sob. "I'm so sorry ..."

"Sorry for what?" Kelly asked, her eyes prickling with worry. "Logan, look at me. Where are you hurt?"

"Kelly!" Sasha's voice was sharp.

Kelly's head snapped up. There in the middle of the hallway stood the shadow. A thin beam of sunlight cut through its middle, rendering its torso invisible.

"There is no body to hurt," the shadow said, licking its smiling lips with a small black tongue, "only soul."

Kelly clenched her fists and she jumped to her feet, but the shadow raised its hand in the same second. The black flames engulfed Logan. His scream tore through Kelly like the clawing hands of the undead. Kelly acted on instinct. She slammed her hands against the air, sending a sheet of air at Logan. The blast sent him rolling into the lockers, but the flames went out. Logan curled in on himself, eyes squeezed shut with pain.

Kelly planted her feet between the shadow and Logan, throwing it the dirtiest look she could muster. Sasha grabbed her wrist so they were facing down the shadow together.

The shadow grinned and called the flames up with a lift of both hands. The hallway burst into black fire, advancing on them. At the same time, Kelly sucked in a breath, ready to slam the shadow with everything she had. The electricity from the fire prickled her nostrils like static shocks. Never letting go of Kelly's wrist, Sasha pulled in a fierce breath of her own.

They threw their hands forwards together. The solid air appeared before them, but the flames would not be forced back. They lapped at the air like it was the glass in a fireplace, climbing towards the roof until a great wall of flames obscured the shadow. Kelly didn't dare let her hands drop. She clenched her teeth as she groaned with effort, willing the solid air to win over the flames.

"Come on, Kelly!" Sasha encouraged.

Her hair pulled backwards as if anticipating the next blast. Kelly drew her hands back, letting the flames inch closer, then she slammed the air again. Her hair was sucked forwards as the blast shoved the fire back at the shadow.

It let out a scream that was enough to set Kelly's teeth on edge. The black fire wrapped itself around the shadow's limbs until it appeared to be made of flames. It flailed in agony, then aimed a vicious throw in their direction. The flames on its arm made a whooshing sound as they were hurled off and struck Kelly in the chest.

Kelly was thrown backwards. The black flames engulfed her in a burning embrace. She rolled away from Logan and Sasha. Visions of classmates dying at the hands of the corrupt flooded her brain. All she could think about was pain and the terrible ache in her heart as she remembered that it was all her fault, all her fault.

"No!" Kelly screamed, crossing her arms protectively and then throwing them open with another scream. She blasted the fire off. It disintegrated in the air.

The shadow lurched closer, limping as if injured, rage in its eyes.

"It's always stronger," the shadow reflected through clenched teeth, "when it's about someone special." It almost sounded rueful.

Kelly didn't know what it meant, but she struggled to her feet, trying not to scream in pain at the burns on her chest. She raised her hands again, her arms dragging with exhaustion. The shadow lurched closer. Kelly tried to put up the wall, but her hands fell through the space between them like it was only air. The shadow was mere steps away, twisting its palms up to bring fire with it.

"I said no!" Kelly yelled, just as Sasha dove to grab her ankle. The second she made contact, Kelly's hands met glass.

The shadow slammed its fists against the shield between them. The glass shivered, the ripple vibrating Kelly's fingers. The shadow glared through the thin sheet of protection, eye to eye. Kelly couldn't make the glass budge no matter how hard she tried.

"It's enough to get us out of here," Sasha called over the roaring fire. "We have to retreat. Can you hold it if I let go?"

Kelly's face was scrunched with effort. Her eyes settled on Logan. He was lying unconscious on the other side of the glass. "We can't leave him."

"We have to," Sasha said. "I'm letting go." She got to her feet.

"*I* can't leave him," Kelly ground out, her arms shaking.

The air between her and the shadow began to tremble with her. The shadow pounded its fists against it again, and Kelly felt the force vibrate up to her elbows. She couldn't hold on much longer.

"Back away," Sasha insisted. "We'll come back for him."

With one last look at Logan, a lump forming in her throat, Kelly took a step back, her hands still up. She promised Logan silently that she would save him. Sasha dragged her away as Kelly willed the wall to hold. When they were far enough to duck out of the shadow's sight, they bolted around the corner and let the wall collapse.

***

They ran until they made it back to the gym, which had

become Kelly's safe place. Her breathing was laboured by now, and Sasha had been pulling her along for several blocks. Her feet were firmly on the ground, unable to fly.

They made it as far as reception before Kelly collapsed on the cold floor and crawled behind the front desk to hide. She rolled onto her back, her chest burning and stinging. Sasha bent over her, pulling aside scraps of Kelly's shirt to assess the damage. Kelly hissed with pain as the cloth peeled away from her skin. She squeezed her eyes shut. The images of death that went along with the burns flashed behind her closed lids. Tears stung her eyes.

"I wouldn't even be in this mess if I'd stopped the Shadow when I first met it," she mumbled.

"And how would you have done that?" Sasha asked as she finished clearing Kelly's burned skin of fabric.

Kelly rolled her head from side to side. "I could have told someone. I could have told Hazel." She gave Sasha an anguished look. "I went my whole life blocking out the fact that I could see ghosts. I never knew that Hazel could too. I ignored everything. I let so many people die."

Sasha frowned, sitting back on her heels. "We're not talking about this shadow, are we? Tell me, how old were you when you first saw one?"

Kelly tried to shrug, but winced instead. "Four?"

Sasha's smile was all sympathy. "And what was a four-year-old going to do about an evil Shadow?"

"But when I was older, I could have—"

Sasha cut her off with a shake of her head. "You're playing a game you can't win. If you could have done differently, you would have. Stop blaming yourself and start blaming the one who actually did the killing. The shadow. None of this was your fault."

The lump was back in Kelly's throat. "But—"

Sasha's hand cupped Kelly's cheek, the only part of her body that was safe to touch. "This was not your fault."

Kelly's lips twitched, an argument waiting on the tip of her tongue. Sasha only shook her head, already denying the silent words. Kelly's eyes filled with tears, and she had to close them against this new pain. She shook with grief and guilt as the tears began to fall. Sasha's words were like a healing balm, an awful, painful balm that could extract the infection.

Sasha sat with her back against the wall and stroked Kelly's hair. The tears rolled down Kelly's temples. It felt like they would never stop.

Eventually, however, Kelly wiped her face and let the base of her palms rest over her eyes.

"I'm sorry," she said. "We've wasted so much time."

She tried to sit up, but Sasha stopped her with a hand to her forehead for lack of an unburned shoulder. Kelly was surprised by how difficult it was to push against.

"You're more injured than you know," Sasha said. "You can't go after that shadow like this."

"It's just skin," Kelly said.

Sasha shook her head. "We don't have skin here. It's your soul that's damaged. You need time to heal."

Kelly twisted away from Sasha's hand and sat up. The world seemed to sway.

"But then Logan ...," she said. "His soul ..."

Sasha hesitated.

"We have to help him!" Kelly cried.

"Kelly, you could barely maintain that wall between us and the shadow at full strength. If we go now, we'll be heading straight for our deaths. Or worse."

Kelly bit her lip. She didn't know how long Logan could last with the shadow torturing him.

"Rest," Sasha insisted. "It's the only option."

26

Chapter 26: Hazel

Hazel felt the blood drain from her face. She grabbed the door and shut it so fast it slammed. Jen yelped from the kitchen, but the ghost woman outside called, "It's Riley!"

Hazel was already bolting the lock, but then she heard the man's voice.

"Yeah, it's me! Hazel, Kelly's in danger!"

Hazel was digging out her phone to call 9-1-1, but the mention of her sister made her fumble the phone.

"What are you doing?" Jen asked, rounding the corner. "You scared the life out of me!"

"The shadow's gone!" the man insisted. "I had to possess Ray to get out of there. I swear it's me."

Jen's eyes popped. She grabbed Hazel's arm with both hands and dragged her away from the door. "Is that *him*?"

The man went on, "Listen! The Shadow this summer, it turned into a spider! And Kate and I killed it with its chains in the motel, and you from the hospital. How would anyone else know that?"

That stopped Hazel in her tracks. As Jen pulled out her own phone to call the police, Hazel put her hand on Jen's wrist.

"Wait," she said.

"You're joking!" Jen hissed.

Hazel crept towards the door with Jen clinging to her arm, trying to drag her back.

"If you're really Riley," Hazel said, a threat in her voice, "what kind of shadow possessed you?"

"An anger shadow," the man said immediately. "You killed it by not letting it take me. The ropes stretched in too many directions, and it burst into shreds. We landed in the pool, remember?"

"Hazel, you can't entertain this," Jen insisted.

Hazel was wracking her brain for more information that only Riley would know, but the female ghost spoke up this time.

"If you can't trust him, trust me," she said. "I know about your visitors the other night."

"What visitors?" Hazel tested her.

"The Mediums who came to your bedside."

Hazel repeated this to Jen, and they stared at each other in silence for a moment.

"How do you know about that?"

"They were friends of mine. They were friends of Ray's, too, before he started killing them."

"Who's Ray?"

"The man who attacked you. But this isn't him anymore. It's Riley."

"H-how is that possible?" Hazel asked skeptically.

Ray's voice answered: "The shadow was holding me hostage. Or my soul, I guess. But it left to go after Kelly on the other side, so I was able to possess Ray. I came to warn you that Kelly needs our help."

Hazel and Jen stared at each other in consternation.

"What do I do here?" Hazel whispered.

Jen raised her hands and shoulders in an 'I don't know' gesture. "We can't let him in."

Hazel ran a hand over her face. Then she raised her voice to ask, "Why do you think a shadow is after Kelly?"

There was a pause on the other side. "I met her a few days ago. It—it turns out I'm a Traveller—it's this ability to see into the other side. Through a door. And I met her through a door. And the shadow has been crossing back and forth through these doors, so it met her too."

"He's trying to kill all the Mediums," the woman said.

"To close the doors," Hazel said as the memory of what Ray had told her in the graveyard clicked, "because his meals keep getting away."

Jen was frowning, so Hazel passed on what the woman had said.

"So Kate was right," Jen said incredulously. "If it kills all the Mediums and closes all the doors, then all the ghosts here—now and in the future—will be at its mercy. We'll all be ... doomed."

"But Kelly is already dead," Hazel pointed out. "Why would it want to go after her?"

Ray's voice answered: "Sasha, a ghost I met, said she's never heard of someone being on the other side. She said Mediums died if they went through their doors. She thought Kelly being there was special."

"But ...," Hazel said, her eyes darting left and right as she put two and two together. "I'm the one who helped her cross over ..."

"So maybe she went through *your* door!" Ray said, and Hazel could hear the awe and conviction in his voice. Suddenly he sounded very Riley-esque. "Maybe she's still there because her door is still open!"

"She's still tied to this world …," Hazel said, her heart twisting.

"And the shadow wants all the doors shut," Ray or Riley said. "She's the knot in the plan! Oh no …"

"What is it?" the ghost woman asked.

"I—I sort of sent the shadow after her." He groaned. "It threatened to go after my mom if I didn't give up a Medium. And Kelly told me she had these defensive powers. I thought she had a better chance …"

Hazel's heart sunk further and further with every word. She turned panicked eyes on Jen, which Jen read easily.

Jen cleared her throat and asked, "What exactly do you want Hazel to do with all this information? How do you expect us to help Kelly?"

There was a long silence on the other side. It stretched on as Jen and Hazel waited, their ears inclined towards the wooden door.

"You can let me cross over," Ray said at last. His voice grew stronger. "I'll go through Hazel's door, like Kelly did. I'll … I'll figure out how to help her."

"You'll die," the ghost woman argued.

"Maybe not," Hazel interjected, her eyes out of focus as she thought. "Last night, in the graveyard, Kelly came back through. Just for a second. Someone pulled her back before the door could break. Before I could die." She turned to Jen. "But if I'm safe, the door can stay open. You could help keep watch, right Jen?"

Jen squeezed the ends of her hair, hesitating. "Aren't we messing with things we don't understand? I mean ... Kelly is on the other side. That's supposed to be it. We're not supposed to cross that line." She lowered her voice to a whisper. "If that *is* Riley, you could lose him *and* Kelly. And ... we can't let him in the house, just in case."

Hazel nodded. "We won't let him in. But Jen ... if our souls are all at stake, and if Kelly's really in trouble ..."

Jen sighed. "Then you have to do something." She turned to the hallway and hollered, "kate!"

Hazel jumped and clutched her heart.

"Yeah?" Kate called from upstairs.

"We have a situation!"

***

Within minutes, Kate was filled in and prepared to join Jen in standing guard over Hazel. The three girls seated themselves on cushions while Ray settled on the step outside. Knowing it was the right thing to do, Hazel texted Riva to let her know something was going down. She asked her to distract Jermaine from coming over too soon. In classic Riva form, she replied, "Of course. Be careful." Hazel smiled at the phone.

"First," Ray's voice coached, "you have to relax. It's almost like meditating."

"That's what I do to help ghosts move on," Hazel confirmed. "Makes sense."

It took a few minutes to relax enough. She found herself playing with the tassels on the seam of the cushion.

"Do you see my door?" he asked.

Hazel opened her eyes, but there was nothing there. "No."

"She's not a Traveller," the ghost woman said. "She won't be able to see it."

"I saw it when I almost died," Hazel pointed out.

"No dying," Jen snapped, and Hazel had to laugh a little.

"As long as I can see Hazel's, it won't matter," the man said. "Keep trying, Hazel."

But no matter what Hazel did, she couldn't seem to relax enough, and the longer it took, the more she worried about Kelly. She pretended she was alone in the hallway, listening to her breath flow in and out like waves on sand. She tried progressively relaxing her muscles, from her toes up. She felt Kate shift beside her, and their knees touched. Hazel felt something change, like the room had grown.

"There!" Ray's voice said. "I see it!" But his excitement fell away at the same time as Kate shifted again. "Oh ..."

"Hold on," Hazel said, maintaining her concentration. She put her hand on Kate's shoulder.

"Good!" Ray said. "Hold it there!"

She and Kate exchanged a glance.

"You must be good luck," Hazel said with a laugh.

Kate flashed a joking smirk like she'd always known that. Then they both gasped. Riley had walked through the wall beside the backdoor.

"What?" Jen cried.

"It's Riley," Hazel said, her jaw dropping.

"Oh good," Kate sighed. "I thought it was a shadow."

Hazel could see Riley as clearly as if he were standing in front of her in physical form. He had dark circles under his eyes, and his shoulders were slumped with exhaustion.

"You look terrible," she said.

Riley huffed. "Well, I've seen better days." Then his face broke into a smile. "It's good to see you, Hazel." He jerked his thumb over his shoulder. "I know you're not the biggest fan of that guy, and neither am I, but can you spare a blanket for him while I'm gone? It's freezing out there."

Hazel repeated this and Jen reluctantly went to find a blanket. She tossed it down from an upstairs window, still refusing to open the door. Ray wrapped himself up while the ghost woman looked on.

"So you can't see the doors?" Riley asked.

"I can see the usual one," Hazel said, pointing to the backdoor.

"Huh," Riley said. "I can see mine and yours."

"Wait ...," Hazel said, trailing off.

"I don't like the sound of that," Jen said.

"If–if Kelly is still on the other side because she went through my door, and you're about to do the same ... can't I go through your door?"

Riley shifted on his feet. "I don't know ..."

"You can't even see it," Jen protested. "How could you go through it?"

Hazel reached out her hand to Riley. "Maybe if Kate can help me call up a door, Riley can help me travel through one."

Jen bit her lip as she watched Hazel's outstretched hand. Riley took it in his, and pulled Hazel to her feet. Hazel's body collapsed behind her.

"Hazel!" Jen cried, catching her before she could hit her head.

Kate had the wherewithal to grab Hazel's hand before the doors could vanish. Riley and Hazel stared at the scene in silence for a moment, unable to communicate with the girls.

"Do you want to go back?" Riley asked.

Hazel didn't want Jen to talk her out of going. Her heart was already light at the prospect of seeing Kelly again. She shook her head. There was no going back.

"We're doing this."

Riley indicated to a door that overlapped the house door. It was a perfect match. A blue light shone through the open crack.

"That's my door," he said.

Beside it was Hazel's door. Hazel set her jaw and nodded at Riley. They traded places, then pushed open each other's doors. Together, they stepped through.

27

Chapter 27: Hazel

For a moment Hazel thought they had simply walked into the backyard. Then she noticed the silence. There was no whooshing sound of traffic in the distance, no neighbours chatting. No ghost woman or Ray waiting for them on the front step.

Riley stuck a hand back through the door and a grin spread across his face. "We did it!"

Hazel mimicked him and was relieved to see that it worked. If everything went well, they would be able to go home.

"So," Riley said, clapping his hands together. "The last time I saw Kelly, she was by an indoor pool, but she was headed to Hillcrest to check on you."

Hazel winced. She did not want to go back to the graveyard. "There are a couple pools we can check on the way over. The first one is that way."

The first step they took made Hazel pause. With her mind on the pool, it was like she had called it towards her, or her towards it. The world seemed to turn closer to her destination.

"Whoa," Riley said.

"What happens if we run?" Hazel grinned.

It took no time at all to get to the first pool. Hazel realized this must be what it felt like to be a ghost. Now that she had her bearings, she realized it was more like flying than the world turning. And it was fun.

Since Kelly was not at the pool, they hurried to the next location, Riley beginning to lag after all his running earlier that day. Hazel went in to find a deserted reception area where the light from the windows fell short of the front desk.

"Hello?" she called. "Anyone here? Kelly?"

A woman with short dark hair leapt up from behind the counter, making Hazel swear.

"Who are you?" the woman demanded.

At that moment Riley caught up, and his eyes popped at the sight of the woman.

"Sasha!" he said at the same time as she said, "Riley?"

Unlike Riley, she did not look pleased to see him. "Oh no! Oh, I'm so sorry, Riley. What happened to you?"

"Oh, no," Riley echoed, waving his hands as if to dispel her worries, "it's not like that. I'm not dead. I'm travelling."

Sasha's lips parted. "But how?"

"Turns out if you go through another Medium's door, you can visit here." He inclined his head towards Hazel.

"Are you ...?" Sasha asked, her eyebrows rising incredulously.

"I'm Hazel."

Sasha sucked her lips in like she was trying to hide her smile. "There's someone here who would love to see you."

She motioned for Hazel to follow her behind the front desk. "Brace yourself though: She's not in great shape."

Hazel came around the corner and saw a figure lying on the floor with a tattered shirt and burns all over her chest. Her eyes were closed. Hazel's breath caught in her throat. She would recognize that chestnut hair anywhere.

"Kelly!" she gasped, dropping to her knees at Kelly's side.

Her sister's eyes opened and landed on Hazel's face. Confusion drew her brows together. "Hazel?"

Hazel's throat seemed to have closed up, so she seized Kelly's hand and held it between both of hers. Kelly stared at their hands for a moment, then sat bolt upright.

"It's really you?" she asked, her forehead creasing with hope.

Hazel nodded, shaking a tear loose. It ran down her cheek, but before it could slip off her face, Kelly had thrown her arms around Hazel's neck. She almost knocked Hazel over.

"I thought I'd never see you again," Kelly choked out.

Hazel squeezed her eyes shut, gripping her sister as tightly as she dared. A sob escaped her.

When she eventually tried to pull back to get a good look at Kelly's wounds, Kelly refused to break the embrace. Hazel laughed through her tears, soaking up her sister's warmth.

"I missed you so much," she whispered.

Kelly pulled back then and the girls hastily wiped away their tears, laughing at the mirrored gesture.

"What happened to you?" Hazel managed to ask.

Kelly looked down at her burns, which Hazel saw had changed from red and oozing to pink and raw.

"I guess I can fix my shirt now," Kelly said, and just like that, her black t-shirt was back to normal.

Hazel stared in amazement. She threw a look over her shoulder at where Riley and Sasha looked on. Both were beaming.

Kelly caught sight of Riley then. She grinned in welcome. "You found her." Then her smile vanished, and she seized

Hazel's shoulder. "Wait, are you dead?"

"No," Hazel chuckled. She explained about Riley's ability and how Kelly going through Hazel's door had led to her current state.

Kelly let out a long sigh of relief, like a mystery she had been pondering for a long time was finally solved.

"So that's why the shadow is targeting you," Riley said. "It needs to close your door."

Kelly looked down at the burns that were visible at the neck of her t-shirt. Hazel realized the shadow had done this to her. Hot rage bubbled in her chest.

"Let's kill it," she said.

28

Chapter 28: Kelly

In the dark grass outside of the high school, Hazel whispered, "So what kind of shadow is this?"

"What do you mean?" Kelly whispered back. They were hiding behind the same tree she had touched on her first day here, studying the black windows of the school.

"The first shadow was a fear shadow; Riley's was an anger shadow. What's this one?"

Kelly thought for a long moment. On the walk over, Hazel and Riley had shared how they had killed two shadows together. Then they had formed a plan.

"Guilt," Kelly said finally.

"Guilt?"

"It said my guilt over you was delicious," she told Hazel. She remembered how the flames had made her see the victims of the corrupt attack, and the pieces fell into place. "And another time it said it's better when it's about someone specific."

"So how do we starve it?" Sasha asked. "What's the antidote to guilt?"

"Forgiveness?" Riley said after a pause. "Self-forgiveness?"

They stood silent in the shadow of the school, each of them pondering their past mistakes. Kelly cringed. It seemed an insurmountable task.

"Well, there's one we can put to bed right now," Hazel said, giving Kelly a gentle elbow. "You don't need to feel guilty about me."

Kelly gave her an uncertain smile.

Hazel grinned and clapped her on the shoulder. "Seriously."

Kelly huffed out a little laugh. "It's not that easy. But I hear you." She straightened her spine. "Okay, if we're going to do this, let's do this."

They crept through the halls of the school, their shoes squeaking on the hard floor. Room after room they searched, but eventually they found themselves back in the lobby. Riley raised and dropped his empty hands. Everyone looked at Kelly.

She hesitated. "I have an idea. But it might be nothing."

She led them out of the school, crossing her fingers that she was wrong. In just a few blocks she stopped.

"What are we doing here?" Hazel demanded, a hint of aggression masking the fear Kelly knew was there.

Kelly swallowed as she scanned the dead-eyed windows of their Gran's old house. The house the shadow had once tormented them in. She turned to the others, keeping it in her peripheral vision.

"There's something I haven't told you. Something the shadow said about Logan." She took a breath and plunged on, "It said it couldn't take his soul because he used to be the core of a shadow. He was tainted. And that's why he couldn't go on."

Hazel's face went pale. Her eyes landed on the house. "You think he's *the* Shadow?"

"I—I hope not," Kelly hurried on. "But … Logan couldn't remember how he died. And this whole guilt thing got me thinking. The shadow took him to the school to torture him, but it wasn't *Logan's* school. And when I got there, he said he was so sorry and I couldn't understand why. But I found him right where … right where I died. I think the shadow was making him remember."

Hazel's nostrils flared. "So we kill him too."

"What? No!" Kelly cried.

"Kelly, we're talking about *the Shadow*. He killed hundreds of people! He killed you!"

"But he wasn't in control!"

"How do you know that?" Hazel argued.

"How do you?" Kelly countered.

Hazel stared at her open-mouthed, like she couldn't believe what she was hearing.

"We can't kill an innocent person. We don't need that *guilt*," Kelly said pointedly.

"Okay, okay," Sasha said, stepping between them. "One thing at a time. We need to take down the bigger threat first."

They backed down, Hazel folding her arms, and Kelly falling silent.

"So why here?" Riley asked.

"This is where the Shadow tormented us after the attack went down," Hazel said, a dark look in her eye. "And where it reaped a lot of souls."

Kelly nodded. "More memories to make Logan guilty over."

Squabble aside, the sisters exchanged a look and moved as one to the front door. Kelly knew by the set of Hazel's jaw that her fearless sister was terrified to go back inside. Her own stomach was an explosion of nerves. She wiped her sweating palms on her jeans. They walked up the steps to the front door. With one last steadying breath, they passed over the threshold and into the living room. The broken front window was covered with plywood. There were no mattresses on the ground from when the girls had slept here. There was no furniture left at all, just the shell of a house, an urn awaiting ashes.

Kelly raised her voice. "I'm here, shadow. Come out."

The shadow stepped through the wall to the kitchen as if waiting for her invitation. It grinned its wide-mouthed grin. Even the peach fuzz of hair on the back of her ears stood on end.

"You brought friends," it said in its gravelly voice.

"I brought shadow killers," Kelly retorted.

The shadow eyed up Hazel and Riley. "So these are the Mediums who killed my kin?"

No one bothered to answer. Kelly and Riley called up the hooks and chains that stretched between themselves and the shadow. In one sudden movement they seized them with both hands. Sasha put one hand on Kelly's shoulder to lend her power, and one hand on the chain. At the same time, Hazel grabbed Riley's. The shadow stumbled forwards with the strength of their effort. It let out a roar that echoed throughout the house like a caged bear.

Sasha and Kelly shifted to the far side of the room, forcing the shadow into the middle of a tug-of-war. The shadow grabbed the chain that emerged from its chest and screamed in Riley and Hazel's direction before it turned its face on Kelly. The malice in the shadow's expression chilled her blood. Something was coming.

Black fire burst to life over Hazel and Riley. They screamed in agony and fell to their knees, dropping the chains.

"No!" Kelly screamed.

The shadow inhaled like it was smelling something delicious, a smile spreading across its face. Kelly dropped her own chain and slammed her hands against the air. She blasted the shadow down the hallway, sending Hazel and Riley crashing along with it. They came to a thunderous halt near a gaping hole in the floor of the adjoining hall. Hazel had harvested the wooden floor to barricade the house against the corrupt.

The fire went out like a candle. Kelly staggered as the effort, paired with her earlier wounds, took hold of her.

The shadow rose like a prowling beast. "I can do this until there's nothing left of them," it warned.

Hazel and Riley were on their feet again, glaring and wincing as they renewed their grip on Riley's chain. Kelly glowered at the shadow. It made a *tsk* sound and the flames erupted over the other two again. Hazel fell to her knees, and Riley screamed in agony, but this time, neither of them released the chain. Kelly and Sasha didn't let their anguish go to waste. They wrenched the rope, and a tear ripped across the shadow's chest. A shred of black smoke escaped into the air, curling like burned paper.

"Stop it!" Riley screamed at the shadow.

"Kelly," Hazel sobbed, and Kelly heard the apology in her voice.

"No guilt!" Kelly shouted. "You did right by me, Hazel! Don't you dare even think about it!"

Black electrical burns climbed Hazel's neck like tiny vines, but Hazel managed a smile. The flames suddenly flickered. There was another ripping sound, and the tear in the shadow's chest expanded. It roared again, shaking the floor under Kelly's feet. The flames rekindled, engulfing Hazel and Riley entirely.

Kelly had no choice. She dropped the chain and slammed her

palms against the air. This time, Hazel and Riley hit the far wall, and Kelly heard a shriek as Hazel slipped sideways and fell through the gaping hole to the basement. Riley tried to catch her arm, but he was off balance, and she pulled him headfirst after her.

"Hazel! Riley!" Kelly cried.

The shadow looked down into the basement, smiled, and lit it on fire.

"No!" Kelly screamed in horror.

She went deaf but for the sound of white noise in her ears. She felt like she was falling and falling and would never stop.

A scream of wrath tore at her throat. She charged the shadow before it could react, slamming the air again, and pinning it to the wall. Eye to eye, she put all her weight behind the sheet of air, trying to crush it, but the shadow resisted.

"You killed them," it ground out. "They're dead because you brought them here."

Kelly felt like her insides were on fire. "They're dead because you killed them." Through clenched teeth she spat, "I will not feel guilt that's rightfully yours!"

She felt Sasha's supportive hand on her shoulder as she caught up, but Kelly's energy was dwindling. A bead of sweat ran down her temple. The shadow grinned and slid into the wall behind it, making its escape. Halfway through, it jerked to a stop. The shadow dropped its gaze to its chest. The chain had reappeared.

Hazel stood in a hollow in the middle of the fire, her hair dancing in the heat, the chain wrapped around one arm. The other supported Riley.

"We thought it was forgiveness," Hazel called. "But it's not just that."

The shadow growled as Kelly's heart soared with relief and pride.

"I've been funneling your energy since you tried to kill me in the cemetery," Hazel taunted. She yanked on the chain. "You tried to make me believe I was responsible for Riley's death. But then I heard Kelly's voice and everything reversed. How does it feel to have someone feed off you for a change?"

"Oh," Sasha breathed. "She's an Empath."

"It doesn't matter," the shadow said, locking eyes with Kelly. "I can outlast you."

It seized a new chain that stretched to Sasha and jerked her forwards.

"Sasha!"

They had brought her right into the shadow's clutches. With her right hand holding off the shadow, Kelly raised her left to slam against the air. It struck Sasha and sent her through the walls as Kelly intended, separating her from the shadow.

Her power was split in two directions. Kelly's arms shook with the added drain. She knew the shadow was right. How could they tear it apart with only one chain? She wished she could slam it out of this world and lock the door behind it. Kelly gasped.

"Riley!" she yelled. "There's a door at the library. You need to call it up!"

"I can't," he said. "I can only call my door."

Kelly shook her head as she gritted her teeth against the shadow's pushback. "This door is yours. It's all of ours. It pulls us like a magnet. Feel it!"

There was a moment of silence from the basement, then Riley said, "I can feel two."

Kelly hesitated as the shadow pushed the air between them,

forcing Kelly back a step. She didn't know which door Riley should use.

"The dark one" came a hoarse voice behind her.

Logan had stepped out of the spare bedroom. His skin was raw and bleeding, his hair burned off. He was using the doorframe for support, and even this seemed to cost him all his energy. Kelly's heart seemed to freeze in her chest as if she were the one dying.

"The dark one!" he called louder, his voice cracking.

A flash of silvery light emerged from the basement. Looking down, Kelly saw the door lying flat in the air. Riley's outstretched hand, much like her own, held it there even though it was out of reach. Inside the door was the same deep black she had seen before, darker even than the shadow's flames. As her exhaustion grew, its promise of nothingness tugged at her stronger than ever before.

Kelly returned both hands to the air that trapped the shadow. She pushed, tilting it towards the hole in the floor. The chain jerked as Hazel added her force and sapped it of energy. The shadow seized for a split second as if electrocuted. Its heels slid towards the edge. Kelly leaned against the air, her whole body on an angle, adding all her weight.

Then one of the shadow's feet slipped off the edge. It tumbled backwards with a cry of alarm. The sheet of air between them shot overhead with nothing to stop it anymore, and Kelly lost her balance. She fell forwards, but Logan dove on his stomach and snatched her hand. She twisted in midair, her shoulder stretching as the shadow latched onto her foot. Half its body hung through the black door, where it began to flake away and meld with the night.

"Kelly!" she heard Hazel cry over the roared agony of the

shadow.

"Keep pulling!" she shouted back, even though the pressure pulled her too.

She looked up at Logan, whose suffering was obvious as he clung to her hand with his burned and blackened one. Even as the terror of nonexistence clenched her stomach, Kelly felt both pity and gratitude well up in her heart. They had to get rid of this shadow. For everyone's souls.

She relaxed her hand like he had taught her. It became intangible and ghost-like, and it slipped through Logan's skin. She fell. Her heart flew into her throat as everyone screamed and the shadow clawed at her leg.

Just when she should have disintegrated into nothingness, Kelly crashed. Then hands were all over her, checking to see where she was hurt.

"What—what happened?" she asked, disoriented.

"You let go, you—you rockpile!" Hazel cried, still inspecting Kelly for wounds.

Above them, the door had disappeared. Logan was running a hand over his face. He beamed down at Kelly, looking delirious with relief. She felt her face grow hot as she smiled back.

"No one's going to check if I'm alright?" Riley grumbled, extracting himself from under Kelly.

Hazel buried him in a hug that sent them both rolling.

"Your timing was incredible!" she hollered.

"Alright, alright, get off me, you cornball," Riley said with a laugh.

Then Hazel was back, squeezing Kelly so tight she thought her burns might scream in protest. Instead, they cooled and healed.

"What's all the shouting? Is everyone okay?" Sasha was

back, leaning over the hole to see the trio in the basement. The grinning faces were all the answer she needed. "It's over?" she breathed, tears sparkling in her eyes.

"It's over," Riley repeated. His smile was so wide it made his eyes water too.

"Come on," Kelly said, and she climbed invisible stairs of air back to the upper level.

When she looked back, Riley and Hazel were staring, dumb-founded. She doubled over with laughter at their expressions, then coached them on how to fly. Before long everyone was upstairs again, congregating in the living room.

"This is Logan."

"Hi," Logan said, raising a hand.

Kelly spotted Hazel's wary expression as the others intro-duced themselves, exchanging congratulatory handshakes.

"Welcome to my home," Logan joked.

Hazel stiffened at that, and even Kelly caught her breath for a moment.

"This is where you've been staying?" Kelly asked.

Logan nodded. "It felt familiar at the time. Of course, I understand why now. So maybe let's get out of here." He let out a nervous laugh.

Kelly loved that laugh. "Good idea."

"We have to get back to our bodies," Riley said, nodding to Hazel. "Let's head that way."

So the group made their way back to Hazel's house, the sisters chatting nonstop all the way. Kelly was ecstatic to hear that Di and Hazel had become friends and expressed her jealousy that she couldn't join them.

Eventually they made it to the backyard, where Kate was diligently waiting on the other side, keeping the door open for them. To Kelly, Hazel's portal was still purple.

Before it was time to say goodbye, Hazel drew Kelly aside.

"Are you sure about him?" she asked, inclining her head towards Logan. "I mean ... he's the Shadow. He killed you."

Kelly watched Logan laughing with Riley. She shook her head. "No, he's not. He was a victim as much as I was. As much as Riley's dad was."

Riley looked up at the mention of his name. "Wait ...," he said, "if Logan was a shadow, but he's here now ... doesn't that mean my dad could be here somewhere too?"

"I—yes, I guess it's possible," Kelly said, looking out towards the mountains she had yet to cross.

Riley's eyes glossed over with possibilities.

"If I can find him, I will," Kelly promised. "And we'll get him and Logan all healed up so they can move on."

Riley bowed his head, overcome with gratitude. Logan flashed Kelly a smile.

"Riley," Sasha said hesitantly, tucking her hair behind her ears, "will you tell Ray I love him one more time? I know he—"

"Of course, I will," Riley promised.

Sasha pulled him into a hug. "And get him to share the Medium group with you. You can learn a lot from them."

"I will."

"Okay," she said, breaking away. "I'm so sorry this happened to you. But thank you for everything."

At last, it was time. Riley and Hazel approached their opposite doors.

"Ready?" Hazel asked Kelly, who needed to return through Hazel's door in order to come back through her own.

Kelly shook her head. She glanced at Logan. "I'm not finished here yet. And someone has to protect this place, in case another shadow gets ideas."

Hazel frowned and opened her mouth to argue, but Riley spoke up.

"That's smart. And then, when we die," he indicated to Hazel and himself, "one of us can take over. We can pass it on to other Mediums and take turns."

"But—we could live to be a hundred," Hazel argued, eyes on Kelly.

Kelly smiled at that. "I hope you do." She waved Hazel over for another embrace. "Now you're not allowed back here until then. But I expect a visit through the doors now and then."

"You got it," Riley said, burying his hands deep in his pockets.

Hazel held on a moment longer. Kelly didn't want to let her go either, but she knew Hazel needed to get back to her body, to her life.

Just before they separated, Hazel whispered into Kelly's hair, "I'm so proud of you."

They pulled apart with shining eyes.

"See you soon," Hazel promised.

"But not too soon," Kelly grinned.

Sasha waved goodbye and flew off in a burst of soft rainbow colours as she headed to her afterlife. Then, with a final wave, Hazel and Riley walked back through their doors.

29

Chapter 29: Riley

Hazel jolted awake in her body to screams of alarm from her friends. Riley watched with a smirk and a glow of happiness. They helped her sit up on her cushion in the hallway. At that same moment, the front door opened and Riva burst inside.

"Dad's coming up the driveway," she announced, hurrying into the back hall. "I couldn't distract him any longer. Are we good? Is everything okay?"

They all looked at Hazel. She grinned. "We're better than good."

Jen let out a breath so long she must have been holding it the entire time.

"Riva," Hazel said, catching hold of her hand before she could run off to help her dad. "I'm sorry about before. You were right. I'm still getting used to all this." She gestured at the house, meaning living with roommates and a girlfriend, as well as going to university and dealing with ghosts. "I'll get better at balancing it all. I promise."

"Okay," Riva said, a smile lifting the corner of her lips. "And

I'm sorry I didn't speak up before."

She squeezed Hazel's shoulder and hurried to hold the front door for her dad. Riley slipped outside as Jermaine walked in and asked, "What are we all doing back here?"

Riley figured he had only a few minutes with Ray before Riva's dad had him arrested. Ray was still wrapped in a blanket on the step, his head nodding.

"Hey," Riley said.

Ray's eyes snapped open, but he didn't have the energy to rise. "How did it go?"

"Good," Riley said. "The shadow is gone. And Sasha was able to move on."

Ray bobbed his head, trying to hide his pain. Riley passed on Sasha's messages, and collected the information for the online Medium group. Before long, the sound of sirens poured down the street. Ray sighed and got heavily to his feet.

"You'll go with them?" Riley asked.

Ray nodded. "I ... I convinced myself I was doing what had to be done. But next to what you managed ... No, I have to do my time now. I owe it to my old friends ... and I have to make it up to Sasha."

Riley sighed. "Good luck, Ray."

"Good luck, Riley," Ray returned.

Riley strode around the corner of the house, giving Ray his privacy as the police descended. It was time to go. He called up the cord that stretched to his body, and almost cheered when he saw it was back, blue as before. He followed it home.

30

Chapter 30: Riley

Seventy-one years later

Riley knocked on the wall outside the hospital room, his age-spotted knuckles a colourful contrast to the bland wall.

"Riley," Hazel welcomed him from her bed, her voice hoarse.

"Good to see you," he said, grasping her hand in both of his. He nodded at two of the other women gathered around her bed. "Kate."

"Riley," the old woman said with a wink.

Beside Kate stood the young Medium Hazel had adopted. Audrey was not so young anymore and had even brought a granddaughter of her own. The blonde six-year-old was nestled comfortably in her arms.

Hazel let out a sigh that became a hacking cough. When she recovered, she said, "Well, let's get on with this. We've all said our goodbyes."

Riley nodded again and settled in the chair beside her bed, his knees popping on the way down. He squeezed her hand as Kate rested her own on Hazel's other shoulder. Hazel closed her eyes, her breath laboured.

In another moment, Hazel stood beside her body, looking at the two doors they had called up together.

"Auntie Kelly!" the little girl cried, beaming.

Kelly and Logan stepped across the threshold, hand-in-hand. They looked exactly the same as ever, untouched by age. Kelly gave the little girl a glowing smile. Logan started making silly faces with her.

"Alright, alright," Kelly said genially, pushing him towards the other door. "Hazel's waiting. Take care, everyone!"

The room was filled with well-wishes and final 'I love yous' to the couple and Hazel. Kelly called up a third door: her own. At the last moment, Hazel and Kelly put their foreheads together, grey hair touching brown.

"Job well done, Kelly," Hazel whispered.

"I couldn't have done it without you," she whispered back.

Riley watched them go with a bittersweet joy in his heart. He remembered the day he had called up the door to Kelly's world, and she had finally said, "We found him." He and Elisabeth had sat cross-legged on the floor in front of that door for hours, saying everything they had ever wished to say to his dad. It turned out Liam had also been a part of the online community of Mediums, not because he had any power, but because he had been seeking support for Riley. He really had been a great dad.

Riley wiped a tear from his eye at the thought of how much he owed the two sisters. The doors disappeared, and Hazel's heart monitor flatlined. He reached across Hazel's body to give Kate's hand a comforting pat before he groaned to his feet.

Kate smiled through her tears and nodded him off. Then Riley hobbled out, already looking forwards to the next changing of the guard.

Epilogue

Hazel

When Hazel stepped through her door at last, she found herself in the middle of the street she grew up on. She was still old, but when she took in a gloriously smooth breath of fresh air, she felt younger than she'd felt in years.

Glancing to the left, she watched as Kelly and Logan emerged in a whirl of muted rainbow colours. The water-like air in the doorway rippled behind them. Their colours swirled around each other as if caught in a breeze. Then they flew down the street, twisting and dancing on the way to their long-awaited afterlife. Hazel couldn't stop the smile that spread across her face.

She decided to spend her first day here doing her favourite activity as a young woman: running. Running, that is, on this magnificently crisp air.

About the Author

Nicole MacCarron is an accident-prone Canadian from BC's Fraser Valley. The accidents started at 8, when she rolled off the top bunk and broke her arm. In pursuit of her Education and English degrees, she nearly broke her neck and back. Nicole currently teaches kindergarten and dreams of returning to Ireland (where she once broke her cheekbone in two places). She is a firm believer that any misadventure can be turned into a great story. As such, most physical pain depicted in her novels comes from a place of experience, and helped to make it all worthwhile.

Interested in supporting this Indie author? Please leave a review on Amazon, or join Nicole MacCarron's mailing list to receive a <u>free short prequel to *Hazel's Shadow*</u>. To get your free short story and to find more books by Nicole MacCarron, go to the website listed below.

You can connect with me on:

- https://nicolemaccarron.com
- https://twitter.com/MaccarronNicole
- https://www.facebook.com/maccarronnicole
- https://www.instagram.com/writersarereaders
- https://www.tiktok.com/@nicolemaccarron

Also by Nicole MacCarron

Hazel's Shadow
2020 Semi Finalist for the Kindle Book Review Awards: Young Adult category

Zombies roam the streets. Ghosts roam the halls. Can one teen psychic survive?

Hazel longs to forget the soul-sucking shadow only she can see. But when the shadow raises an army of corpses, she would rather die than risk her sister's soul. Before the undead attacked, Hazel's life was simple: look out for Kelly, make the wrestling team, hide her crush, and keep her ability to see ghosts a secret. But now, the sisters and their classmates are cornered in the very house where the shadow lurks. As the night unfolds, Hazel struggles to juggle her secrets and keep everyone alive. But how can she tell her friends she can see ghosts when her own mother didn't believe her? And how can she confess her feelings for Jen when rejection feels as dangerous as the undead army trying to kill them? Despite her uncertainty, Hazel may be the only one who can save them all— if she can survive long enough to discover the shadow's sinister purpose.

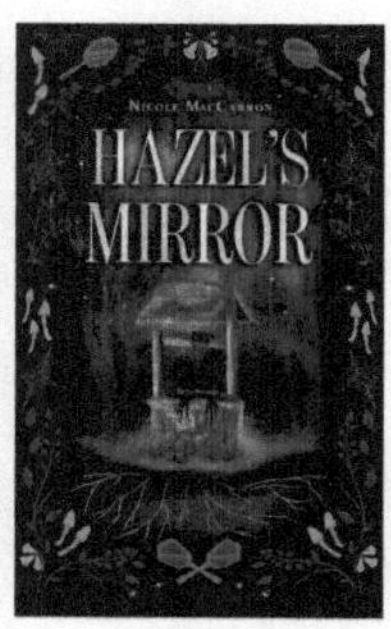

Hazel's Mirror

Hazel thought a weekend away would be fun. She didn't count on getting haunted.

After last year's massacre, Hazel has spent a year suppressing fear and grief. So when the opportunity arises to get out of town and support her girlfriend in a basketball tournament, Hazel is quick to pack her bags. The weekend takes a dark turn when a mysterious boy begins haunting her and Hazel realizes they may have something sinister in common. As their worlds gradually intertwine, Hazel finds temptation among new supernatural abilities. Thrust into the unwanted role of mentor, she must test her new talent to discover if it will save them both, or destroy the last remaining people she loves and unleash her worst nightmare.

www.ingramcontent.com/pod-product-compliance
Lightning Source LLC
Chambersburg PA
CBHW060716190726
48289CB00002B/713